America Hates Me But I Still Love Her!

37499

STAMFORD 325.73 OZTU
Ozturk, Umut.
America hates me but I
still love her! /

**STAMFORD VILLAGE LIBRARY
STAMFORD NY
12167**

America Hates Me But I Still Love Her!

Umut Ozturk

iUniverse, Inc.
New York Lincoln Shanghai

America Hates Me But I Still Love Her!

Copyright © 2005 by Umut Ozturk

All rights reserved. No part of this book may be used or reproduced by any means, graphic, electronic, or mechanical, including photocopying, recording, taping or by any information storage retrieval system without the written permission of the publisher except in the case of brief quotations embodied in critical articles and reviews.

iUniverse books may be ordered through booksellers or by contacting:

iUniverse
2021 Pine Lake Road, Suite 100
Lincoln, NE 68512
www.iuniverse.com
1-800-Authors (1-800-288-4677)

ISBN: 0-595-34724-X

Printed in the United States of America

FOR MY MOTHER AND FATHER

Contents

Chapter 1 1
Chapter 2 2
Chapter 3 3
Chapter 4 7
Chapter 5 11
Chapter 6 15
Chapter 7 25
Chapter 8 29
Chapter 9 32
Chapter 10 36
Chapter 11 41
Chapter 12 46
Chapter 13 49
Chapter 14 55
Chapter 15 57
Chapter 16 61
Chapter 17 64
Chapter 18 71
Chapter 19 73

Chapter 20	78
Chapter 21	81
Chapter 22	87
Chapter 23	92
Chapter 24	95
Chapter 25	97
Chapter 26	103
Chapter 27	107
Chapter 28	112
Chapter 29	120
Chapter 30	122
Chapter 31	124
Chapter 32	125
Chapter 33	126

Acknowledgements

There are many people to thank. I like to start with my brother's Kanat and Bulut. You guys are the best brother's a person can possibly have. I am looking forward to getting old with you. My little sister Rain, I love you. You are my little princess.

Off course there are those that are dear to my heart besides family. I have to start with my two best friends. First one is Steve Colbet. Steve and I have been through a lot. Steve, you are definitely a hero of mine. I will cherish our friendship forever. If you ever need anything in life I will always be there for you. Steve if it were not for you I would have never finished this book. Thank you for being a wise guy. My second best friend is Brian Brazil. Thank you for becoming very important part of my life. I am looking forward to visiting England with you and meeting Keira.

To Mr. and Mrs. Brazil, I aspire to be like you both. Thank you for being there through the good and the bad. Mr. Brazil you are an inspiration to me. I hope as I get older I could turn out as classy and as caring as you. Thank you for all of your help. Mrs. Brazil you are awesome. I sincerely do hope that one day I could marry someone that is similar to you.

Mr. and Mrs. Creel thank you for accepting us as whom we are. I am looking forward to uniting with you once again at your house. I am definitely looking forward to your delicious iced tea over a great conversation.

Off course not but least, I could never forget my college roommates, J.B. and Shad. Thank you for being real with me every second of the way. You guys are awesome.

1

It had been forty-two days now. I had made an arrangement with the United States Homeland Security forty-two days earlier that I would not leave their Louisiana Jurisdiction and that I would check in every Wednesday telephonically. In the past forty-two days a lot of things had changed. I had picked up all my family, some of my belongings and left the great state of Mississippi. Homeland Security had no idea of this. To them I had done nothing wrong and that I was still present in Biloxi. I was still checking in on Wednesday's by phone even though I was in Minnesota. But it was my cellular phone that was getting the job done. My cellular phone had a Mississippi area code and as long as homeland security received my phone calls from a Mississippi number I was safe. By the sixth check in, I had disconnected my cell phone and disappeared into a Minnesota winter.

2

I don't know where one can begin. Especially, if that person is writing about him or herself. In my case I am writing about myself. My name is Umut. People in my hometown of Biloxi know me as Turk. The reason I don't know where to begin is simple. This is the first time in my life that I am going to be brutally honest about my family and me. The question is an ordinary one; is it possible to be actually honest? Or, do I hide things from the reader to make myself look good? I thought about these two questions for a long time. I know it is part of human nature to lie to ones self and just continue lying as you go. Eventually with time those lies that I have been telling myself and other lies starts becoming true in my own mind. The truth or reality becomes distorted. As a result, I don't know what is true and what is not. How long can I deceive myself? This is a hard question to answer. But I can answer it. I have been deceiving myself for fifteen years now and frankly I am tired of living a lie. I assure you this will be the most candor thing that you could read about a person or a family. Therefore, sit back, relax and enjoy the ride.

3

I moved to Biloxi from Turkey in 1990. At the time, I was twelve years old. The reason we moved to the United States was due to my father being part of U.S. Air forces and Turkish Air Forces exchange officer program. At the time my father was a young Major. My fathers name is Mustafa and my mothers name is Gaye. I definitely like them a lot. Both of them are Turkish. We will come to this interesting fact later on. For an average twelve year old I was definitely not in the same level as my peers. Even as a young kid growing up I was very weird. Rich people would call this eccentric. Since I am poor, I call it weird. I know that you used to know some kids that were very big dork's or kids that did not fit in while you were growing up. I am that kid. I was the nerd and the loser that everybody picked on. In middle school even in Istanbul I was a nerd. As I was growing up I never had any friends. Except my brother Kanat. However he does not count. He was obligated to be my friend. Kanat and I did not like the same things growing up therefore I was all alone, Don't get me wrong, I always loved being by myself and not being part of a group. However, being alone gets to you after a while.

When I moved to Biloxi, I did not know how to speak any English. Since I lived in Kessler Air Force Base I had to attend Nichols Middle School. The school was predominantly black. Let's get this straight, I am not a racist and not all people that live in Mississippi are racists. People that don't live in Mississippi have a pre conceived notion that just because they watched a movie about Mississippi that they know the Magnolia State, but guess what? Not all things that you see on television are true. Things have changed and Mississippi in my mind is one of the greatest places you could grow up as a kid. The reason I made the statement about school being ethnically diverse is simple. Never in my life until age twelve that I made any contact with a black male or a female that was my age. In Turkey my father had a good friend that was a black officer in the American Air Force. His name was James. James had a daughter with braided hair that was younger than me. That was my only contact with a black person. As one can see, the first day of school was looming towards me. Off course I was about to experience very serious form of cultural shock. I don't know about my brother but I was scared. Imagine being twelve and having a very limited vocabulary in English; thank you, yes sir, no sir, yes ma'am and no ma'am. On that hot August night I could not go to sleep. I was dreading that black Monday. I was thinking as any other twelve-year old would think at the time, what am I going to do? How many times do I have to say thank you? Or where will I go? What will I eat? Would I like the food? Who would I meet? Would they make fun of me? Would I get roughed up? Would a bully dump me into a garbage can? Off course now looking back all these thoughts seem so embarrassing.

Thank god my father knew how to speak English. He was the only one in the family at the time that was fluent with this great language. However, his fluency was not an American English but more of the British English. That dreadful morning rolled around. We hopped in to our overpriced Buick Regal Limited and went to Nichols Middle School. If you know Biloxi at all, the Main street area of Biloxi is the worst part of town. That is where Nichols Middle School was located. It was on Main Street by Yankee Stadium. Driving through this neighborhood, I was wondering if this is the best America can offer to my family. By the time I got to school I was a nervous wreck. I swear I had to use the restroom at least ten times while I was in pupil accounting. My father went on to the principal's office and talked with a huge man. I promise, at the time he looked like a pro wrestler to me. He was an enormous black man. A couple minutes later my father came out of the room with this giant. My father turned to us and said, "I am leaving." He had to go to work. We gave him a hug and he left. As he was leaving, I wanted to start screaming from top of my lungs, "don't leave us here! Please don't leave!" But I did not scream nor said a single word. I just watched him get into his Buick and leave. Black Monday had begun.

Eventually the time came. The principal said a couple of things to my brother and I. Principal called for one of the pupil accounting students. They took us to our classes. Needless to say Kanat was in sixth grade and I was in the eight. We would not see each other, until the E.S.L (English is Second Language) class. As I walked to my first class I could feel the butterflies in my stomach. I wanted to throw-up. With my unfortunate luck the first class of the day was American History. I did not know anything about American History. Why would I? I did not even know anything about Turkish History. Even if I did, I would not be able to express my knowledge. The teacher was this gorgeous black woman. Her name was Ms. Jackson. She asked me my name, and I told her. She could not pronounce it. I did not care because I could not pronounce her name either. Another reason I did not want to correct her was that I did not want to get more attention on myself. She made me sit in front of the class. Since I am sitting in the front, I could feel the eyes of my future friends looking at me all at one time. Maybe I was being paranoid. But I doubt it. As this beautiful woman spoke, the dizzier I got. All of my classes on that day were very similar to my history class. Dizzying giant roller coaster ride. My body was a dart-board and my class mates glares were darts. It was painful and scary. My last class of the day was ESL. Here I met a young Vietnamese teacher name Mr. Pham. Again, being from turkey, this was my first speaking contact with a Vietnamese person. I distinctly remember the conversation;

Mr. Pham smiled at me and said, "hi Umut!"

I responded like a moron, "thank you."

Looking back I feel so stupid now. I don't know why. As the next day came about, I decided to play sick, it was to no avail. My parents were not born yesterday and they were not buying it. My father even made a stupid rule. He said, "there would be no Turkish spoken in the house during the weekdays." That included my mom and my two brothers. A couple of weeks went on and nothing had changed. I was still the same dumb kid. No improvement in my English. However I had become friends with someone. His name was Espy. Espy always laughed at me. Even though I did not understand what he was saying I laughed back. Everybody was scared of Espy. You are probably wondering, how does he know if everybody is scared from Espy? I tell you how, sign of fear in people are universal. Knowing this important fact, I decided to hang out with Espy as much as possible. Since I was with the bully, it meant nobody would mess with me. Smart strategic move on my part. Wouldn't you agree?

I was in America now for a month and half. That same roller coaster ride kept on repeating itself on each day. One day, I came to school and Espy was not there. I went on with my day. A couple of days went by and he was still absent. I became worried. Was he hurt? Was he sick? Did he move? Why didn't he call me? Wait I know why he did not call. He did not have my phone number. I wondered, what if Espy does not come back? I thought if he did not come back, I was in deep shit. I will become an open target for everybody. On Thursday, he was back. He missed three days of school. I was thrilled and relieved to see my best friend. I tried to ask him where he had been, but I did not know how. But, he showed me a piece of paper that read, OSS. I did not understand the meaning of those three letters until my English got better. Out of school suspension for getting into a fight was the reason Espy had missed school. That day was one of the better days I have ever had. Espy was back. I was ecstatic. At the same time it was one of the saddest days in my young life. Out of nowhere Espy laughingly said, "Umut, you dress like a girl." When Espy said that I was very confused and dejected. I knew what he meant by girl but I did not know what he meant by "dress like". I was mad because I knew it was an insult. However I did not know what kind of an insult it was. When I got home I asked my father in Turkish about my friends comment. I did not care about his stupid rule at the time. Dad realizing the severity of the situation responded to me in Turkish. I broke his rule but I did not care I was crying. He explained to me what Espy meant. After that explanation, I realized maybe that is why people always stared at me. My clothing was feminine in color according to American fashion at the time. But this is who I was, at the time I was Turkish. This is how middle classed Turkish citizens dressed. I had to make a change on my appearance and clothing. That night we went shopping at BX. I picked out what ever I wanted. The next day I went to school with my new clothes and my first pair of Air Jordan's. People were still looking at me but the darts were plastic now. It did not hurt me as much. Everybody including Espy loved my Jordan's. For an instant no matter how brief it was, I actually felt like I belonged. I felt as if I was cool. It was all because of my friend Espy.

As months went on, I started liking school. Exactly four months went by and I realized people around me learned how to talk Turkish. Everybody at school knew and understood what I was saying. One day my youngest brother Bulut who is five at the time came home elated. Bulut told my father that everybody in his school knew how to speak Turkish. Bulut was in kinder garden. My father just looked at Bulut with a smile and said, "it is not that everybody learned Turkish, it's just that you learned how to speak English." It was a great moment at an early age. All of us were learning the language at a very fast pace and liking everybody around us in the process. I was actually gong-ho about going to school. My eight-grade year flew by. I found out from dad that I would be attending Biloxi High School the following year. It was not fair. I wanted to go back to Nichols. I asked Dad, "why am I so unlucky?" He laughed. I was jealous Kanat got to go back to Nicholl's. At the same time I was scared and confused all over again.

4

It was the winter of 1995. I was seventeen and a senior at Biloxi High School. I was in student council and the president of the Fellow Christian Athletes. In five short years, I went from not speaking any English to being fluent at it. The reason for my rapid climb was rather childish. In my mind I had to fit in. By that I mean, I had to be an American like my friends. I did not want anybody to talk about me and say; "you know he is that Turkish kid." I wanted people to see me as who I was, Turk.

I was pretty athletic, especially in soccer. Playing high school soccer kind of made me a star around Biloxi. I was about 5 feet 11 inches, average height but I was quiet skinny. I weighed about one hundred-thirty pounds. Everybody knew who I was. I was popular now. The recognition kind of made me pleased but at the same time it was hard. Being a star soccer player had its downfalls. Everybody expected me the score every game. Other teams started to learn who I was so they decided to concentrate on shutting me down. Because of opponent concentration on me, I was not able to score as much on my senior year. Being a weak kid did not help the matters at all. I was easily getting tired during games. I was just out of shape. My senior season went by super quick. At the time I was feeling empty like the way I feel know. I did not know how to express myself so I had to do something different. I no longer wanted to play soccer. It was my first love. But, I had to let it go. I decided to get into coaching soccer. I had all the credibility in the world. Who would not want their eleven and twelve year old to be taught by someone that really knows what they were doing? This is a rhetorical question. I do not need an answer.

I went home that cold winter night, trying to find out how to get into teaching kids to play soccer. Honestly, I made about twenty calls, left messages and nobody returned my calls. The emptiness in me grew, I was really disgusted with the world. I thought I was the unluckiest person in the world. A week went by and I tried again. I finally got in touch with the Biloxi Soccer Organization. This gentleman from Biloxi Soccer Organization told me, he had a team but he did not know anything about soccer. He asked me if I could help. Hearing this made me ecstatic. Off course I would help. This was my big break. I automatically volunteered. The anticipation of meeting this voice made me real nervous. That night I could not go to sleep. To this day, I still remember my first encounter with this man. The name of the voice is Jim. I called him coach Jim. Coach was a little shorter than me but as skinny. He was from New England. Coach Jim was about my father's age with a childish face. He was somebody that smiled a lot. I liked that a lot about him. It made me very comfortable. Since, I was working on my people skills, I decided to emulate him. As a seventeen-year old, my father was the only man I ever tried to be like. I decided to smile as much as possible and be like coach Jim. On that first day as he spoke to me, his smile made me become calmer. He showed me bunch of kids at the middle of the field and told me that they were our team. As I slowly approached them, I could feel my heart pounding in my head faster and faster. I did not know how I was going to make it through my first practice. I met all the kids. They were wonderful.

Our first season went by in a fly. Our team name was the tigers. Since our colors were gold and purple, we named ourselves after the Louisiana State University Tigers. We had our own team song. The purpose of this song was to take our minds off running while we were running. We ran and we sang. The song went something like this,

> We are the tigers we are the bestWe are ahead of all the rest
> The other teams are all has been
> We just like to play and win
> Our coach seems to yell a lot
> But, we show him what we got
> Our coach stands upon the grass
> He just likes to kick our grass.

For some reason I have a sudden memory loss. I can not remember the rest of the song to save my life. Don't you hate that? It is in the back of your mind somewhere but since you are thinking about it, you can't remember it. As soon as you quit thinking about it, you remember it. Sometimes life is funny like that. Like I was telling you earlier, my first season was rather quick. The tigers were the league champions, going undefeated with a record of, fourteen victories, zero defeats, and four ties. It was definitely a miracle year. We went on to Jackson for the state championships. We got our heads beat in. But, I was not disappointed. I knew the kids gave their best. Coach Jim and I were happy with the results we achieved that year. At the time it was my calling. I was meant to be a soccer coach. People still stop me, when I go to the soccer fields and tell me, "You should go for it and become a coach." I would just smile to that statement like Coach Jim would have. Thank them for their complement and move on. Let me tell you something about Coach Jim, he is definitely one of the classiest guys I ever met. To this day I still try to imitate him and his demeanor. Coach Jim is one of the reasons that I am in love with Boston sports. I love my Red Sox, my Patriots and off course who could forget Ray Bourque and the Bruins.

During my first year of coaching, there was this one kid on the tigers that always followed me around. Wherever I went he was right behind me. For a long time I thought he was stalking me. My stalkers name Brian Brazil. The bad thing was, not only he followed me around but his little brother Sean that was not playing on my team me, started following me too. I had my first encounter with being stalked. I was famous. I had my own stalkers. Brian was this all-American kid with blonde hair and blue eyes. Only problem was that he was a horrible soccer player. He absolutely stunk up the room. He was clumsy, uncoordinated, and always fell on the ground when he ran. I played him only the required two quarters but always went out of my way to talk to him, cheer him up and encourage him. I knew at the time, if I screwed up with his confidence now, this kid would hate soccer because of me. As the year went on I watched him trying to copy me. This boy could not run worth of crap but here he was trying to do different soccer moves and falling on his ass. It was funny to watch. But, I did not laugh. I just smiled. This is what the equation looked like. (e) Means' to emulate. Brian emulated Umut. Umut emulated Jim.

(Brian (e) Umut (e) Jim)

It was funny how things worked. We both had somebody to emulate with the exception of our fathers.

The years went by. It was six years later now. Brian was nineteen years old and I was twenty-four. It was the district championships. In order to advance out of our district to move on to state championships, you have to finish first or second in your district tournament. April 13th of 2002 in the semifinal game we were down three to one with fifteen minutes to go to our arch-rival Mercy Cross. In Biloxi people that went to public school at Biloxi High School hated the preppy private school kids from Mercy Cross. Even though some of these kids were friends, when it came to athletic events they were bitter enemies. Mercy Cross was up 3-1 on us at halftime. I looked around and saw my boys. They were all upset, because their season was coming to an end. I told everybody to keep your head up and keep on fighting. Than the miracle in Hattiesburg happened. With fifteen minutes to go, that clumsy kid from Biloxi took over the game like there was no tomorrow. On a corner kick, he passed the ball to my youngest brother Bulut, Bulut stopped, looked, and hit a perfect shot to the upper ninety with no angle and made the score 3 to 2. We were still down. Now with only ten minutes to go. This gawky kid I was telling you about earlier went around several people gave a pass to Zack. Zack took a shot and we tied the game at, 3-3. The fans were going crazy. It was pandemonium. The teams that were getting ready to play their semifinal games at the same field as us were cheering for the underdog. Nobody could believe it. Brian knew exactly how much time we had left. Whatever he had left at his gas tank he was about to spend it now. With five minutes left in the game and score tied, Brian received the ball on the corner flag gave a pass to Stefan, Stefan went around one person and took a shot. It was in the net, the score was four to three now. We were winning. But, Mercy Cross has one more push left in them. They came down the field took a shot. The ball hit the cross bar. I thought they tied the game at that point. In our next possession, with a minute left, Brian received a pass from Bulut at midfield and went on a full sprint to the house. He went around exactly four players and put the ball in the back of the net. The whole place was going crazy. It was pandemonium. Kids jumping up and down, parents hugging parents. Brian's hands were up in the air. Our fans on our sideline kept chanting for him. "Zizou, Zizou, Zizou, Zizou….". Zizou is French international Zinedine Zidane. As he was dribbling the ball to the goal, all I could see was myself as a high school senior taking it to the house. I was in tears. Even as I write about it know, I still get a little choked up. Brian became the best player on Mississippi Gulf Coast. He will be attending college this fall to play community college soccer with four of his teammates that played for me that year. Brian (Zizou) went on from being absolute worst player to an absolute best player in six short years. In the process he became my best friend. Obviously, I would not even trade him for the real French sensation, Zidane. Coach Jim and I are still very good friends. Nothing has changed, he still is the graceful gentleman that he is. If it were not for his friendship and his great personality, there would absolutely be no Zizou memory to write about. I am grateful that I was able to meet and cherish Coach Jim's friendship. Go Red Sox.

5

In 1992 my father's tour of duty at Biloxi was over. Our family had to make a decision. We had two choices. We could go back to Turkey to our life that we came from or we could stay here and continue the life that we were accustomed to. My mom Gaye being the strong woman that she is, decided her and the kids will stay. My father would go back to Turkey. Dad would continue his life as a career military man.

By 1992 my father now was a Lt. Colonel. On August of 1992, he placed all of us, which included my new born baby sister Rain River Ozturk on one of the base inns and returned to Turkey. Our apartment on pass road would not be ready for another two weeks. That meant we would have to stay on base for two more weeks. My father was gone. It was now my mom, Kanat, Bulut, Rain and me.

First year was real easy for the kids. But it was rather hard on my mom with four kid's ages ranging from fourteen to early infant. We were kids therefore it was not complicated for us at all. Dad would be back whenever he could for visits. First year for me flew by. Our phone bills were ridiculous around three to four hundred dollars a month. Since my father was a Turkish officer in Turkey now, he was making Turkish money. He was sending almost thousand dollars a month and that was really hard to live on. We were officially poor compared to the life we used to live. Dad used to make five thousand dollars a month. However we the children did not care. We thought our life was exceptional. Our apartment had a pool. That was good enough for my siblings and I. I was living it up. I loved America. Everybody knew me at school now, I was no longer the outsider. I was inside the room with the rest of the kids looking outside now. Just two years ago, I was that kid at Nichols who was always outside looking in. I was no longer a greaser. It was a big change for me.

In 1993 I turned fifteen and my father was still in Turkey. The money was scarce. One thousand dollars was not enough. I had to get a job. I got a job working in the mall at an ice cream store. It was called Dellie's Yogurt. The owner was a real nice Colombian guy. It was my first interaction with a Colombian. His name was Lois. Him and his wife owned it and operated. Hell, I did not know why I got hired. I did not know anything about ice cream. I had no previous experience. I did not even like ice cream. As I got older I realized maybe I got hired because I kind of looked like I could be a Colombian. I thought that was pretty neat. Working at dellie's was not hard at all. The first two weeks were very frightening. I did not know anybody that I worked with. I felt outside those two weeks. I felt like I was the only greaser among bunch of socials. But now I was a grown man I could handle it. I told myself, "Quit being a big baby." I was the man of the house now. I made all the money. I tell you what was hard about working, my schedule. I would get-up at six in the morning to go school. At three o'clock, I would go to soccer practice till five. After that I would have my mom rush me to the mall in our cheap broken down ford escort. I would work from five thirty to nine thirty. I would get home at nine forty five, take a shower and go to bed. It was the same routine for about a year.

I will let you into a little secret. I hated that escort. It was the ugliest car that I have ever seen. It was old and navy blue. I still remember asking my parents, why did you buy that stupid car. My mom was always sweet about my complaints. Whenever I was being obnoxious like that, she would smile and say, "would you rather not have a car at all?" I guess the glass was always half full for her and the opposite for me. I was making $4.25 an hour working thirty-hour weeks. Even though thirty hours is nothing now, it was hard then. For a fifteen-year old, thirty hours seemed like an eternity. I was making extra four hundred dollars a month now. I was giving every penny I earned to my mom. Our income went up from a thousand a month to fourteen hundred a month. It was still not enough. The rent was $425, the phone bill $300 and utilities $200. That leaves about four to five hundred a month for everything else. I know what you are thinking, "gosh use the phone less." I know. But, we had to talk to dad. We missed him.

My mother was always a house mom. Mom never had a job in her life. However being a house mom is not easy at all. It is a profession by itself. She was legally allowed to work in this country. But how could she? Her English was not well. She had a new baby girl and three young boys to take care of. Only thing she knew how to do was to take care of her house and her kids. I give her a lot of credit. Our apartment was always in immaculate condition. Our clothes always ironed. We were pampered. Even if mom wanted to work, none of the kids would want her to. We were so use to her being at home and taking care of us. Kanat, Bulut, mom and I were able to work in this great country of ours. Off course so was Rain River. I was jealous of Rain. Why? Rain could do whatever she wanted as she got older. She was the only person in our family that could actually run for the presidency. Rain was the only one that could actually take advantage of all the great things America had to offer. I knew that. Knowing this made me despise Rain for a long time. Now looking back, I know it sounds childish. It was not fair. Why her? Why not me? Why couldn't mom and dad create me in America? Why couldn't I run for presidency? I was an unlucky bastard. I was more American than most of these actual Americans that were born here. This included my little sister. I bled red, white and blue. I appreciated and loved America. I hated people that said negative things about America. I was always very quick to verbally whip anyone that did not show loyalty to this beautiful nation of ours. Think about it, you make your money here and then you put down this country as soon as something did not go your way. I disliked people that were unappreciative. It was not right. However I understood it was one of our rights as citizens to bitch and moan. I could not choose where I was born. If it were up to me I would have asked to be born in Biloxi like Rain. I guess some people are cursed from birth. Not only this country was the only thing I knew, the great state of Mississippi was my home.

Things got rougher for the Ozturk household as the year 1994 rolled around. My father was not sending thousand a month. It was eight-hundred dollars a month now. According to the inflation in Turkish economy his salary went down. I never understood what the hell that meant. I never thought money (lira) in Turkey would loose its value. In my eyes, that would never happen to the U.S. dollar. So we had less money to get around with now. My father and mother were fighting a lot more over the phone now. It was over money I thought. But that was only half of the problem. Mom wanted dad to be here with us. I could not blame her. We all missed dad. Dad's star was on the rise in Turkey, rumors were if he stayed in the military several more years, he would someday be a general. That was very important for my mom. To be known as a general's wife, this was my mom's eternal goal. However, after a while that no longer mattered to mom. She wanted her husband in Biloxi with the kids and her. My father now had a life decision to make. Do I retire? Do I go to America?

My father retired from the Turkish Air Force after putting in twenty-five years of his life into it. As a retirement bonus the government gave him eighteen thousand dollars and a plaque. I thought this plaque must have been a joke. I have received prettier plaques by just playing soccer. Even now thinking about that plaque gets me angry. He still receives eight-thousand dollars every year from the Turkish government. Think about this little fact; twenty-five years equals to eighteen-thousand dollars in retirement bonus. If you do the math for twenty-five years of service equals roughly eight-hundred dollars a year. So dad received eight-hundred dollars for the each year he served in the Air Force. I made more money at the ice cream store than what the Turkish government was paying dad.

To this day it still pisses me off. If dad were an U.S. Colonel retiring, he would at least be making in the ballpark of three thousand a month. Same service, same effort but only two thousand dollars more a month.

My country knew how to treat people right compare to dad's country. Dad's country was two hundred years behind in civilization, compare to my country. I hated the treatment people received over there. When Dad arrived in 1994, he was in bad shape. I guess anytime you leave the love of your life, you will look that horrible. Dad was same height as me and weighed about one hundred and fifty pounds. His young face slowly giving into wrinkles of old age. That was the first time I realized the man was hurting. Everybody was happy in the house now. The Ozturks was a family again as a whole. We had our whole life ahead of us. We did not know what was going to happen in the future. But, we did not care. We were together now. I know looking back at things now, future was going to change my outlook in life forever.

6

Even though dad was with us, his eight-hundred dollars a month did not help us at all. I know you are wondering why can't this grown man go out and find a job. I tell you why, the U.S. Government would not allow him to work. Once Dad would apply for a working permit, he would be giving up his NATO status for good. Everybody in the family was getting older. I was seventeen now. Kanat was fifteen years old. That was the good news. It meant now we had two people in the house with a job. Kanat worked in the mall at steak and burger. He was a hard worker. It was a hamburger joint. He worked forty hours a week and made roughly around seven hundred dollars a month. Now our family income started to increase. I could not wait till Bulut to start working. He was now nine years old. In six short years he would be the third money-maker of the family.

The fights in our house became larger. It was always about money. As long as I could remember myself, not having enough money always has been the biggest problem in my family. We were never financially stable. I guess that is why I hated money so much. My life kept moving on regardless of the fights. In May of 1995 my high school graduation was nearing. I was about to graduate. I was very proud of my place in my class. Out of three hundred and twenty people, yours truly was about two hundred and eighty something. I never cared about school. It was a place to socialize for me. I did not even know what I was going to do. It seemed like my friends had the rest of their lives figured out. Some of them were going to LSU, some to Ole Miss, some to Mississippi State. Here I was, young stupid kid going to work full time at Grand Casino Gulfport as a valet attendant. I was happy. College was not for everyone. I did not envy my friends, this was the life that I had chosen. I was going to deal with it. Working full time making about ten dollars an hour only meant, less fights at home. I was happy with that. I could no longer stand the bickering at the house. If more money kept their mouth shut, than that is what I would do. I would produce more money.

As time went on as a valet attendant, I started to miss high school. Especially one person my French teacher. I began taking French in my eleventh grade year. My French teacher was a young teacher. He was about twenty-five years old. To me he was cool. Can I speak a lick of French? Heck no! My English was still in progress. But according to graduation requirements in Mississippi, I needed to take two years of foreign language. French was an easy choice to make. I had no intentions of learning Spanish. I wanted to speak the language of love in order to woo young females. Bonjour Mademoiselle!

My first interaction with Mr. M was ordinary. I honestly thought he was a student the first time I saw him. I did not tell him this fact. I did not want to embarrass him. But, my two years taking French was like trying to jump out of a car that was going hundred miles an hour on the interstate and expect to survive. French was unbelievably hard. As my eleventh grade year went on, farther behind I was falling to rest of my classmates. Anytime a student is little slow, (like myself) the student tries to get attention in different ways. My way to cope with my stupidity was easy, I decided to be the class clown. At any given moment I was willing to crack jokes and interrupt the class as much as possible. Being dense, I needed the attention. Mr. M being the genius he is, knew exactly what I was doing. His threshold for tolerance was very high. Every time I would get in trouble, I would never get sent to the principal's office. Instead, I had to come in before school started and sit quietly for thirty-five minutes. That was hell. I would rather get sent to the office. This went on for two years. I never made a grade higher than a seventy in his class. Which is a passing grade in this state. My senior year came and went. As my senior year came to an end Mr. M and I had a little deal. I asked him, "If I make an "A" on my next big test, can I be exempt?" His response, "Yes." I thought it was a fair deal. Make a good grade and miss school the next day. The following morning I came in and took the test. I studied the night before. I must have studied for at least five hours. Next day, I just went in to the classroom and rolled the dice. The test was not multiple choice. It was fill in the blank. I winged it. I knew I made an "A". The next day I got the results. I received an "A+". Mr. M and I never discussed this till my graduation. On my graduation day he gave me a little letter in French. I asked him, "how the hell am I supposed to read this?" He said, "One day you will." I just smiled at him like a moron. I gave him a hug and went on with my life.

I was working the graveyard shift at the casino one night. The weather was horribly cold in December. About four in the morning, I was leaning against the heat lamp and I dosed off. In about twenty minutes I was awaken by a smell of something burning. I did not know what it was. I started looking around and could not locate the smell. Then all of the sudden I felt the warmness of the heat around my neck. My jacket was on fire. I unzipped my jacket as fast as I could and threw it on the ground. I put the fire out on my own. But, it left a big burn mark on my jacket. That night I decided to continue on working my nights but I had to start going back to school during the day. I did not want to become a bum. Not that there is anything wrong with being a bum. If you are happy with being a bum, then all the power to you. Seven months into the real world I started to envy those friends of mine that were at Ole Miss partying. I wanted to be just like them.

I enrolled at Mississippi Gulf Coast Community College's Jefferson Davis campus. It was ten minutes from my house. I did not care about making good grades, but I knew I had to make passing grades to move on to a four-year school. My major was French. I was determined to read Mr. M's note. No matter how tired I was at night, the next day I was at school. I had to get the hell out of dodge and save my life. Since I did not make good grades in high school I had to pay my own way at school. It was expensive. It cost $425.00 a semester. I went none stop for three years. Again, community college is two years for a lot of people but it took me three. I will give you another proof of my slowness. I took two years of French at Jefferson Davis, just enough to understand the letter. The letter by Mr. M's stated that, "If you put your mind into it Umut, you could do anything." It moved me into tears. At that moment I knew I had solved the puzzle. I was destined for greatness and I would not settle for anything less. I told myself, "When I get my four year degree, I will visit Mr. M." That goal lit a fire under my ass. I was inspired. Being inspired is a great thing. It makes you do things that you could never think is possible.

After three years at Jefferson Davis, I knew my time was up. I had to move away from home to finish my education. I enrolled at The University of Southern Mississippi's Hattiesburg campus. Being a full time student and living on campus, I needed to make money and send it home. I immediately became sport official. That was paying about seven dollars an hour. It was definitely better than not making any money at all. I became a resident assistant for the housing department. That guaranteed my dorm and food to be free. I was happy. My job as a resident assistant was easy, all I had to do was to be social and make sure all the freshmen at my floor were happy. Two years at U.S.M. went by real fast. It was some of the most interesting years in my life. Now when I look back, I just have a big grin on my face. There are two stages to my life at USM; first, the Meridian stage and second, the Poplarville stage.

First, the Meridian stage. After three years at Jefferson Davis moving to Hattiesburg was a blessing. I was twenty years old now. I needed to be free and independent. This was my big chance for both. Only problem with living on campus was I did not know whom I was going to live with and piss off. When the time came to move to Hattiesburg in the fall of 1998, I was ready to start my new life.

Fall of 1998 on a Friday, I got to Bond hall. I checked in at the front desk and moved into my room. I was the first person in the room, so I chose my side of the room quickly. All I knew about my future roommate was that his name was Shad from Meridian, Mississippi. I was kind of anxious waiting for him to move in. As the day went on, my anxiety grew. I decided to take a walk around campus. Shad did not move in that day. Next morning I went to eat breakfast. When I came back I turned on the television and decided to watch sports center. Suddenly I heard a door knock, and it was my future roommate. At first glance I could not decide whether he was black, white or Hispanic. It did not matter and I did not ask. Shad was short and bulky. He was about five feet nine inches tall and probably weighed about buck eighty. He looked strong. He was definitely somebody I would not want to fight with. As I helped him move his stuff to the room, he seemed really friendly. I immediately learned he was a sports fan just like myself. We immediately had something in common. The problem between Shad and I was a simple one. He loved the Cowboys. I could not stand the Cowboys (note-Since Bill Parcell's is the current head coach. I am a huge Cowboys fan). I thought, maybe we could work through this little problem. A week went by. Shad and I were getting along fine. We were bonding. Then one day Shad asked me something that I would never forget.

> Shad avoiding eye contact, "Do you mind if a friend of mine stays with us?"
>
> I did not know what to say, "Off course not!"

What the hell was I supposed to say? He was my first roommate and things were going real well. I did not want to mess things up. I thought by saying no, that I would screw up the whole year. Moments later Shad made a phone call and my second roommate came in. I guess he was waiting in the lobby for an answer. His name is Jonathan and he to is from Meridian. Jonathan told me to call him J.B. I was definitely okay with that. J.B. and I automatically kicked off great. I was a big Steelers fan in college. J.B. also was a Steelers fan. I am a big Bill Cowher Fan. This immediately made us friends. That first night J.B. was with us, I can't remember going to sleep. It seemed like we had so much to talk about with so little time. We were trying to learn everything in one night about each other. My Meridian stage officially kicked off in the fall of 1998 when J.B. moved in. Every week on the club night my roommates would ask, "Do you want to go to the club with us?" I would always say no. I did not know how to dance. I was being a big nerd. We also had a regular routine. Every day Shad and I played a game called NFL game day on play station. Shad began a streak of sixty-three straight games over me that fall and continued till the middle of February. Every time Shad would beat me, he did his dirty bird dance. He was trying to copy the touchdown celebration of the 1998-1999 Atlanta Falcons. Every time Shad did the dance J.B. and I could not stop laughing. He was hilarious. The year went by real quick. We were great friends. Our room definitely was the most ethnically diverse room on campus. We had a Turkish person, and two African Americans. Needless to say, this was my first time living with my new brothers. I would tell them this all the time and they would just laugh at me. Shad and J.B. would call me, "Fidel" or "Durango" or "Turkish assassin" for being a little crazy. They had many nicknames for me. I also had many nicknames for them. I called Shad, "Andres Galaraga" the stocky former first basemen of the Braves or "Kirby Puckett" former twins outfielder and off course "The Bear." He was shaped like a bear. Shad hated all of those nicknames. He could dish it out but he could not handle the jokes. I had several nicknames for J.B., "Tyson", "Jo Jackson" and "Bernie Mac". We would pick on each other as much as possible and time would fly by. One day in the middle of February, Shad and J.B. woke me up around seven in the morning.

>I said to them, "what the fuck is going on?"
>
>Shad with his big cat grin, "Fidel, are you ready for your sixty-fourth straight loss?"
>
>I got all cocky and said, "bring it on Kirby."
>
>I turned to Tyson and asked him, "do you want a piece of me too, punk?"
>
>Tyson replied, "you crazy Turkish bastard!"
>
>Without hesitation I turned Tyson's way again, "when I am finished with the Big Cat, you are next."
>
>Tyson smiled and put me in my place, "fuck off Fidel, go to sleep. You know you never beat him and you never will. Quit trying, just go to bed."
>
>He got me all hyper I started jumping up and down on my bed "you next biatttccch."
>
>Kirby frustrated with all commotion, "Enough talking. Let me kick your ass for the sixty-fourth straight time."

I got up with my pink Mickey Mouse sweater on and said, "let's go."

By now, both Kirby and Tyson wanted a piece of the "Turkish assassin." Before the game started Shad decided that he was going to record this beating in order for me to learn from my mistakes. Several minutes later Shad and J.B.s' friends stopped by. Our small dorm room was full now with seven people. Everybody was now wagering money. Odds were simply favoring Kirby by three touchdowns over the Turkish Assassin. Tyson was the bookie for that event. Since I lost sixty-three straight times, I had to change this streak. I was so tired of getting my ass kicked. I did not want to be humiliated anymore. Now was the time and I had to fight back. In the first quarter I went up by two touchdowns by the end of second quarter I was leading Shad 35 to 14. Game was over by virtue of the twenty-one point rule. I was jumping up and down in celebration of my first victory against Bobby Fisher. I was doing Shad's dirty bird dance. I really did not know what I was doing but I was ecstatic. I was screaming like Mohamed Ali when he won the heavyweight championship of the world, "I shocked the world, I am the greatest, I am a one mean man…" Shad's friends including J.B. were making fun of him and teasing him. But also, they were laughing at me hysterically as I kept on yapping. I turned to J.B. and asked him, "Do you want a piece of the new champ?" Off course his response was no. That day none of us went to class. The three of us stayed and ordered Papa Johns Pizza. It was a glorious day.

Throughout the year we had made some great memories. One day, "Jo Jackson" walked in during the exam week without saying a word. He grabbed a baseball bat and out he went. I did not know what the hell was going on. I had a pink Mickey Mouse sweater on. I know "pink," the room was cold and that is the only long sleeve sweater I had. I had to keep myself warm. I decided to get the bat out of his hand but it was to no avail. I followed him to the stairs and started going down the stairs. We stopped at the second floor balcony and looked down. Looking up to us were almost the whole football team. They were staring at J.B. and I. Being the big dummy I am, I was staring at these people like I could take them. I guess they thought I was nuts. I bet they thought, "what male college student in his right mind would wear a pink sweater?" They are right. These people were physical specimens. We would have absolutely no chance against these machines in a physical confrontation. J.B. and I came back to the room, locked the door and just sat. I was horrified. I did not want to be pounded like roast beef by those athletes.

I asked, "J.B. what is going on?" No response!

I asked again "dude, what is going on?"

Silence.

I asked for the final time, "J.B. What is going on?"

I got no response from him. He was in total silence for the next hour. Finally, Shad came into the room. I told him what had occurred. He just laughed about it. Shad turned to J.B. and told him to quit being a big baby.

Shad asked J.B. what I had asked several times earlier, "what is wrong?"

J.B. finally responded. He saw his high school sweetheart that he has been dating for about four years kissing one of those football players. At that moment, seeing this made him realize it was over between them. That broke his heart. If that would have happened to me, I probably would have grabbed a baseball bat and try to do something irrational like J.B. also. Good thing, there were a whole herd of football players downstairs. If not, J.B. could have done something horrible in that second of weakness.

My Meridian stage came to an end after the finals in May of 1999. It was a fun year that went by in a blink of an eye. I am grateful that I had a chance to live with these two different but wonderful characters. The room was for two but we made it work with three of us. J.B. slept on his inflatable bed on the ground. I am glad I said, "yes" when Shad asked to see if J.B. could move in. There were probably fifty different times we threw his bed out of the room. We moved out of our room at end of spring 1999. All three of us carved our initials on a newly cemented ground in front of the Bond Hall and moved ahead in full speed. Not knowing what the future had in store for us. But we knew in our hearts, no matter what happened, we would always be the three amigos.

Second, Poplarville stage. I am a little intoxicated on this Saturday evening. After work I had a Sunkist martini. It tasted like shit, but I indulged it anyway. I am the only person awake in our apartment now. I am listening to some Turkish music that my father put on. It is the first time in a long time, I am listening to something other than country music. It feels weird. But at the same time, the music I am hearing is sad. It is making me sadder by the second. It is peculiar at this hour, I am thinking about the only woman that I have ever loved. Off course I am not counting mother or my little sister Rain. I am just going to call her Poplarville. Poplarville first caught my eye in the fall of 1998 in Hattiesburg. She walked into my life without ever noticing me. It was the first day of class. This goddess strolled in front of my desk and found her seat in the class. I could not take my eyes off her. I had to introduce myself, but I did not know how. Every time the class would meet, we would have the same routine. I would glance at her direction as she came in and she would not notice her admirer. This went on for the whole school year. I know what you are thinking, "what a pudding boy?" I agree. I have never been good with the ladies. Therefore, I was not going to embarrass myself. Let me give you a brief description of Poplarville. She is about five foot ten inches tall and weighed about hundred and twenty pounds. She was a brunette at the time. She had beautiful brown hair that reached to her shoulders. Beautiful face, and a petit nose. Since my nose is very big, I always liked girls with small noses. We established earlier, that I was a little weird. Therefore, the reader should not harp on that matter any longer. You know I am weird and I know I am weird. Lets move on. As my junior year ended I still had not spoken a word to her. My goal that summer was to find a way to break the ice. It was imperative that she knew that I existed.

The summer break went by quick. I went back to school. All of the sudden I was a senior. I had to find out where Poplarville was. I was in disarray. I thought, "maybe she goes to school somewhere else now," or "maybe she already has graduated." I was disgusted with myself with wasting the past school year not even speaking to her. "What if she got married?" "What if she is engaged?" What if she moved?" I was real upset. I made a promise to myself that day, as soon as I would see her, I would introduce myself to her. Being the lucky guy I was, the next day we were in the same class. The routine had not changed. The summer did not help me at all. I had not changed. She walked in, I glanced at her direction, and she moved on without noticing her admirer existed. I decided on a course of action. I would follow her. This was the only rational idea I could come up with at the time. Pretty psychotic, uh! The class ended and I started my way towards humiliation. I was about five yards behind her at all times. I followed her all the way through campus. I am a psycho, I know. I guess she was done with her day. She was going to her car. I saw classmate of mine walking towards us. I had no time to talk to him. However, he stopped and said, "hello" to Poplarville. Than noticed me and said, "hello". The same guy I did not want to speak with just a seconds earlier, suddenly became the most interesting person in the world to me. He was talking to both of us at the same time. Suddenly, he asked us both, "Do you know each other?" We both nodded no. Knowing that was not true, I was a little embarrassed. My hands were sweating and my heart was beating really fast. I never felt this way about a girl before. He turned to her and said, "this is Turk", then turned to me and said, "this is Poplarville." She looked at me and smiled. I melted as she smiled at me. This was the first time she noticed me. So I thought.

Then Poplarville proved me wrong and said, "I think I have him in a couple of my classes." I wryly shook my head in agreement. She said, "Nice to meeting you and went on her way." Instead of being happy for meeting her, I was mad as hell. I should have been looking at the positive, which was she knew I existed. I should have been elated. Instead I was not happy at all. The negative thing was, apparently I had no chance with her. I knew it would never work. Fall of 1999 went on and made way to spring of 2000. Since this being my last semester at Southern I decided to talk to her. One day after class I approached her with a question about class. I acted like I was lost. I just wanted to talk to her. She was real kind, we talked as we walked. Once we got to her car I asked her for her phone number, she gave it to me. I was happy. I was making progress now. Small progress but still a progress. It had only taken me a year and a half to talk to this girl. It again shows us that I am very slow. We started hanging out with each other. We went to see movies together. I had fun. I figured she also enjoyed herself. I don't think I ever asked her if she had a good time. We talked and became friends that semester. We kissed, we hugged and we laughed. In the end I was ecstatic that I finally talked to her. It took me a long time. I admit it. It is better than not talking to her at all. We both graduated with a B.A. in liberal arts on May of 2000. We stayed in touch. She only lived forty-five minutes away from me. I was absolutely smitten by her. I had to see her all the time. Next several years we were never actually together. I always had someone else and same thing for her. But that did not stop us from getting together every chance we got. We were young and stupid. We were not meant to be together and I knew. The realization of being an eternity apart from her tortured me. I asked to be together, but Poplarville did not want me. All she had to do was ask, "I would have been hers forever." But as I said earlier, life is funny like that. It never goes the way the heart desires. Especially for me, we got into many fights because of that. I wanted her and she did not want me. It was the same thing that happened to J.B. I finally realized why Jonathan could have been that mad over a girl. It was a couple of years to late. But I got the gist of it. Rejection is painful thing. When the heart is broken, it is hard for it to heal. The timing was always off between Poplarville and I. We never actually both liked each other in a reciprocal fashion at the same time.

I finally got to a point of no return. My threshold for tolerance for her was no longer there. One day I got mad at her, told her to go to hell. We did not speak for a year. I was miserable. I thought about her everyday. Finally on one evening after a year I gave her a call. We spoke to each other and acted like nothing ever happened. This is how the conversation went;

    I said to the love of my life, "I missed you."

Poplarville responded kindly, "I missed you too."

I said, "I thought about you a lot."

Poplarville again being kind to me, "me too."

I finally said what I been wanting to say for a year now, "I rather have you in my life than not have you in my life at all."

I could feel her smiling on the other end. Several days went by and we made a promise to meet each other and have dinner. She was still as beautiful as the day I first saw her. We had our dinner, acted like we have not missed a beat. I took her to her house and gave her a hug and left. At that moment I knew she was out of my life forever. Even though I would run into her again in the future. Things would never be the same again. She went out of my life just like the way she came in.

7

I graduated with degree in speech communications on May 12, 2000. Can you believe it? I now had a four-year degree. I would have never thought that I could finish college. I always had a low self-esteem. I was never good in school. I guess being in America and wanting to be everybody's all American made me go nuts. It made me want to change. I so desperately wanted to be an American that I would have done anything to feel like my friends. If I could feel more American by going to school and getting a degree than that is what I would do. All I ever knew was America. I was in love with her. I loved everything the flag stood for. It represented people like myself. Immigrants that left their homes in order to chase a dream. Stars on the flag represented many immigrants coming to America two hundred years ago and settling here. Every time I took a trip to New Orleans, as I would pass through Slidell going on I-10, I would see this giant American flag over one of the car dealerships. I would get emotional and teary eyed seeing this flag. I loved America and I was thankful for being in the greatest nation in the world. It is really hard to explain. But this is who I was now. I was an American first and Mississippian second.

After graduating from Southern, I still did not know what I was going to do with my life. I was twenty-two years old and single. I had no where to go. I moved back with my family. If you are familiar with the show Everybody Loves Raymond, my mother and father are very similar to Marie and Frank Barone. Things were always the same at home. At our household there were a lot of laughter. The laughter would turn in to crying, and that would turn into fighting. Fights were always over financial reasons. We did not have any money but we fought over money. It is very easy to fight over something we did not have. Summer of 2000, I got a job. This was my tenth job in the past seven years. I became a waiter at a fine dining restaurant. It was at a casino in the bay. I worked at many different jobs prior to this one. I was a cashier, ice cream man, valet, cook, valet again, dishwasher, video store attendant, resident assistant and a summer camp counselor. This is one job I never wanted to do in my life. I did not want to serve people food. However I quickly found out this was the easiest money I could make. I waited tables at this fine dinning restaurant for eleven months and decided to quit.

I found another job at a fine dining restaurant. It was a family owned Italian restaurant. It was my second time ever waiting tables. The key to getting this job was real uncomplicated. All I had to do was pretend like I knew what I was doing. I had to act, I had to pretend to be an expert as a waiter. Acting came easy to me. Acting led to waiting and waiting led to making lots of money in a short period of time. I was making five hundred dollars a week easily. I had call parties coming in and asking for me. People were coming from Vegas, Florida, Alabama, Louisiana, and asking for me to wait on them. I was an immediate success. The key to my success was I left my tables alone. I did not talk much. I took the tables order and brought them what ever they wanted. They were here to socialize with each other. They were not paying all this money to talk to me. Realizing this made me a great waiter in my opinion.

Even though I was making all this money, the fights continued at home. If you have a household of six people and your income is not enough, fighting will happen. My mom and dad could argue with the best of them. They were real mellow people, but once they got mad, get the hell out of their way. I always disappeared as soon as a fight broke out. I did not want either one of them to come up to me and ask me my opinion. I did not want to be in the middle of it. I did not want to have an opinion about their disagreement. Being the intelligent person that I am, I knew they would eventually make up. If for some reason that I would have an opinion during the fight, it would lead to a cross-examination then to re-cross from both mom and dad. Knowing this and having previous experience in this field, I would keep my mouth shut. No matter how hard they fought I would never have an opinion.

After a year into serving tables, I decided I had to find a job more intellectually stimulating. I am not saying serving tables is not stimulating intellectually. However, after a while it becomes the same routine. Thing's get real boring, people seem real annoying. Everything seems the same and the days are interchangeable. I wanted my life to be more adventurous. I wanted to be like one of those people on television. Obviously waiting tables could not accomplish my wish. Hell, I only lived once. I deserved it. I was going to make the best of my life. That is the best I can explain it. I sure did not want to be an average John Doe. I wanted to be special. One day I came into work and asked Robert our dishwasher, "What is going on?" He smiled and responded, "same shit, just a different day." I had to agree with my friend. That is the best anybody had ever put things in perspective for me. I did not learn that simple fact in five years of college. It is really amusing, who teaches you what in life. Robert taught me more in that one statement than most other people that I came in contact previously. As I was saying I needed change. I decided I wanted to become a lawyer. I started looking into law schools and their requirements. The requirements included a four-year degree, grade point average of 2.0 or higher and satisfactory score on the LSAT (Law School Admissions Test). I already had the first two pre-requisites. I had the degree and the G.P.A. Now all I had to do was, to take the test and do well on it. I tell you a little secret about myself, I have never been good at taking big exams. I always flunk them. That includes the ACT. I started studying for the LSAT. After several months of studying, I decided to take the test.

First time I took the test, I made a 135. That is like making a fifty out of a one hundred. I needed to improve on my test score. I decided to take a course to help me better prepare for the test. It was Kaplan. 144 is what I made the second time. The average score is 150 and I was way below average. I decided against taking the exam again. Who needed the stress? I applied to at least eight law schools in this area. I got rejected by all of them. It almost felt as bad as when Poplarville rejected me. I felt like a total loser all over again. I felt stupid eight times in the next several months. After a while a person builds a callus for rejection. The seventh and the eight-letter did not felt as bad as the first six. I was not complaining or whining. I sure would not blame anybody else for my own stupidity. This was all me. I thought about giving up on law school with each rejection. However, I was the grand son of Husseyin Ozturk. He grew up with no money, no water and no electricity. He taught himself how to read and write. I was not going to give up because I knew he wouldn't. My grand father on my father's side was an inspiration to me. At least I had running water and electricity. I continued telling myself, "this is the land of the free, anything was possible here in America." I continued on researching more law schools. Finally, I found one more that I wanted to apply to. It was the Thomas M. Cooley Law School in Lansing, Michigan. I was a fighter. I did not care if I got rejected again. Eight or nine rejections, it is just a number. This is what I wanted to do with my life. I wanted to be a lawyer. Regardless of what happened with Cooley, I was going to keep my head up. I applied for the fall semester of 2001. Waiting for an answer was hard. Everyday I went to the mailbox and everyday no reply. I was getting pissed off. The anticipation for another rejection letter, just killed me. I said, "maybe this is it, I am destined to be a server for the rest of my life." Not that there is anything wrong with being a server. It is an honorable occupation. It just wasn't what I was meant to do. I was absolutely at an all time low now. The letter that I was waiting for ultimately arrived in November. I did not open it right away. I had to go inside and open it in my room like the previous seven rejections. Before I opened the letter, I said a couple of Hail Mary's to myself. This is what the letter said,

"We regret to inform you,"

I know that you could imagine how the rest of the letter continues. I was rejected for the ninth and final time. But wait, was I just joking? Was I really rejected again? I am just kidding. The letter informed me that I was accepted as a freshman in the upcoming semester. I was ecstatic. I knew this is what I wanted to do, now I had the chance to do it. I was going to be an attorney. No longer was I going to be a poor white thrash. I was ready to make a difference in the world. No matter how little of a difference, I was going to make a difference. I knew I got lucky. If I were anywhere else in the world, I would not have these chances I had here in America. I knew that and I was thankful for being in America. I appreciated her and loved her like a husband. Now I had to find a way to finance my law school education. I knew I would get a couple of bumps on the road before I got to law school. I did not care. I told you earlier, I was a fighter. A weak fighter, but still a fighter. I was not afraid to trade blows with anything or anybody. I could do whatever the next man or woman can do, or do it even better. Over the years that is how I had to program myself. I was still lost but not as bad. At least now, I could see that glimmer of hope at the end of that dark tunnel.

8

Gaye was born in April of 1956. Her full name is Fatma Bedia Ozturk. Her father always called her Gaye for some silly reason. Name Gaye was given to my mom by her father. He did not want to call her Fatma Bedia. It sounded to country for him. He wanted his daughter to have a modern name. Hence that is how the name stuck with her. As a young girl growing up, my grand father and grand mother got separated. When they got separated she was six. My grand parents were twenty-four. Neither one of them was mature enough to take care of a young child. My great grand mother on my grand father's side raised her. My great grand mother lived by herself in Istanbul and that is where Gaye's adolescent years were spent. She was a beautiful little girl. As she grew up, she got prettier. She started resembling Bridget Bardot on her prime. Gaye was gorgeous.

    Growing up was hard on Gaye. As she got to be fourteen years old, she decided to go live with her father in Germany. Needless to say, he was a total loser. However, she needed her father around at that tender age of fourteen. My grand father was already re-married by now. There were no new children from the second marriage. My mother's step-mother was a slut. She treated my mom like crap. She would not let her go outside or let her do anything the average fourteen-year old girl would do. Like a moron my mom stayed in Germany for the next several years. She just wanted to be around her father. I guess that is not hard to understand. My grand father could not even recognize these injustices his slut wife was doing to my mom. He was too busy hearing the sound of the whip cracking on his ass. I never realized what my grand father saw in that ugly woman. Like I said earlier, love is funny like that. In my grand father's case, he was absolutely in love with this garbage. By injustices, I meant no food or snacks. Even worse, she could not even go to the movies with her friends. My step grand mother was very similar to Cinderella's step-mother. Only difference was, my step-grand mother was real. I believe she was jealous of Cinderella's beauty. Being the wench she is, I believe that was one of the many reasons for the treatment mom received.

    At seventeen my mom moved back to Istanbul to live with the woman that raised her. They got along beautifully. They loved each other. They were like sisters. At seventeen she was ravishing. Being a high school senior, she was being chased by all kind of hormonally unbalanced animals. One of Gaye's uncles was a sheriff in Istanbul. He kept a close eye on his gorgeous niece. Times were a little different back than. Man and woman were not equal in Turkey. Even now there are some inequalities. This was the early seventy's. My mom dropped out of high school for a reason that was unclear to me to this day and never went back. This is one thing she always regretted. I assume her uncles did not want to deal with all of these little hoodlums that was after her.

As she got older, prettier she got. Let me describe her a little bit to you. She is 5'9 about hundred and thirty pounds. Very light skin. Brunette, but not quiet a blonde. I could see how guys chased her. From the stories I heard she was a heartbreaker. There was a guy before my father that wanted to marry my mom. He was a military officer. At the time she was twenty years old. I believe they got engaged for a brief period of time. For some reason that engagement never led to a marriage. Her fiancée had left her. He did not want to marry her. She was jilted. I did not know the reason. Her heart was broken. My mom is an emotional person like myself and I could imagine the pain she felt. Gaye being the determined person she is, wanted to marry a military officer. In Turkey being an officer in the military is a prestigious occupation. Since, she still felt the pain from being jilted, I believe she made a promise to herself, one day she would be a Generals wife. She had to lock the memory of this guy in a safety deposit box in her heart and throw away the key forever.

My mother had enough connections through her uncles and aunts to become a flight attendant for the Turkish airlines. Having connections in a country like Turkey goes far. This is one of the reasons I can not stand uncivilized governments. Connections mean more in uncivilized places on earth. Connections actually mean more than qualifications in Turkey. For example, people that can not be pilots in this country because of their eyesight can easily become a pilot with their connections in Turkey. I think that is a horrible way of living. People abuse their power more in Turkey than here. Why? People are more uneducated. That is one of the reasons I can't stand uncivilized nations. Suddenly mother was going through orientation in order to become a flight attendant. Her connections were working. During this time she put a little ad on the paper in the matchmaking section to meet her future husband. I know the reader is wondering, "if she is as pretty as he says she is, then why would she need an ad on the matchmaking section of the paper?" Easy question to answer, for adventure. I could see the logic of that question. However, even beautiful girls have tough time meeting people too. That is how she met my father Kemal through the matchmaking section of the paper. After writing to each other a couple of times, they decided to meet. They met at a deli in Istanbul. My mother was very inquisitive of this new stranger on their first date. She asked him, "what is your occupation?" His response, "I am in construction." The truth was he was lieutenant in the Turkish Air Force. She had no clue of this little fact. They continued seeing each other after their first date. They had their second and third dates. My mother did not care about his occupation anymore. She really liked this dark stranger. When my father told her of what he did for a living, she was in cloud nine. She knew this was the guy she wanted to marry.

9

Once I got accepted at Cooley Law School, I had a little over ten months to get my shit together. I was still employed by the same restaurant. I actually liked my job more now. However, I knew this was a temporary occupation. Realization of things being temporary is real comforting. It felt as if the prison sentence was reduced. I was given a second chance in life. In prison, not that I have ever been to prison, the second chance would be called "parole." Or in some other peoples cases "escape." I looked at Cooley as an escape from the real world for at least another two to three years. I would soon become a parolee. I loved the idea of going to law school.

When I started working in the restaurant industry, it was a little hard. The hardest thing was not having any friends at work. If you ever worked or been around the restaurant business, most people that work at night has very screwed up life styles. By screwed up, I mean people with drug and alcohol problems tend to work at restaurants.

Everybody at the restaurant would go out together almost every night. They would get smashed. They would do some cocaine then do some ecstasy. How do I know this? These same people would come to work the next night and brag about it. I knew these people were not my crowd. I was invited several times by these people but I did not go. I declined the invitation. I had no place among these creatures. Their life and mine did not mix at all. I did not drink nor did drugs. There were two reasons I did not drink. One, I could not handle alcohol. Two, I did not like the taste of it. I don't know why but my tolerance for alcohol was unbelievably low. I had nothing to do with drugs because it was illegal. Here I was at work, surrounded by drunks, drug users, gamblers and drug dealers. It was definitely a culture shock. At The University of Southern Mississippi all we would do was drink and party. Now, at work I was surrounded by all sorts of unbelievably abnormal people. They were not my people. Therefore, I banished myself from the people I worked with. My co-workers did not like me and I did not care.

After a while I was able to adjust to the situation. I just went to work, did my time and left. Like anything else that I have encountered in my life, I have always been able to adapt to the environment that I was in. Work was amazingly easy. I had the schedule that I wanted. I was off Sunday and Monday's. I eventually became friends' with this guy nobody liked his name is Steve. He was the boss. Steve did not do anything except work. I have never seen a guy that worked so hard in my life. Steve worked six nights a week. He came in to work at three in the afternoon and left at three at night. He was working seventy-two hours a week. First six months that I worked at the restaurant, I did not say a word to him. Likewise, Steve did not talk to me either. We both did not like talking much to people that we did not know. One day I was curious about learning golf. I wanted to buy some used golf clubs. I came to work early in order to look at the classifieds. As I was looking at the classifieds to find some cheap golf clubs, Steve asked me, "what are you doing?" I said to him, "I am looking for some golf clubs. I decided to take up golf." He said to me, "I will keep an eye on the paper for you." I said, "okay." The following day Steve true to his word had found me some clubs. They were fifty-five dollars. At the time I did not have the money. He said, "it is a great deal, you better go buy them." I told him I was low on cash. He gave me fifty-five bucks. I went on and bought my first golf clubs. The next day he and I went golfing. My first time playing eighteen holes of golf was at Broad Water Golf Club. I was absolutely horrible. It was a hard sport. I had no clue on what I was doing. All I knew was to hit the ball. I was swinging the golf club too hard and completely missing the ball. I could not make contact with the ball to save my life. Steve gave me the nickname of "Whiff Woods." That day he beat me by at least seventy strokes. He laughed at me for the next four hours. That was the way we became friends. After several months of golfing he became one of my best friends. Because of our friendship, nobody liked me at work. That was the final straw. Everybody hated me. In the past they did not like me because I made no effort to be their friend. Now, they did not like me because I was friends' with the enemy. I did not care. I knew the kind of life all of them led.

The restaurant was a family owned and operated restaurant. Steve's sister and his brother-in-law owned the place. Therefore, like any family owned place, there were a lot's of fights among the family. I kind of liked the fights because it made me feel like I was at home. I was trained to be around altercations. I was an expert on this matter. I knew the employees were gossiping about my friend. If I ever walked by during the process of their gossiping, everybody would quiet down. Those employees were snakes on the ground. They would smile at Steve's face and then talk behind his back. I always hated people like that. I just wanted to beat up people like that. But, I knew better. Violence would never solve anything. It would only lead to more problems. They looked at me as if I was a snitch. Hell, it did not matter what they thought about me. I was a grown up now. Nothing would bother me.

Being Steve's friend had its fringe benefits. I got to chance to eat every night for a little sum of money. Just imagine eating at a fine dining restaurant every night for about five dollars. I was eating fillet mignons, New York strips, veal chops and lamb chops. I was gaining weight. After being Steve's friend for six months I had gained about twenty pounds. My skinny frame was starting to fill out. There were other benefits to our friendship. He and I would go golfing at least three days a week. I did not have any money for this expensive sport. Steve would pay for both of us. For four hours at the golf course, we would shoot the shit. Sometimes during the course of play, I would get so angry that I would start throwing my clubs in the water. He once told me, "Whiff, your clubs that you throw goes farther than your ball." I would get angrier to his teases and eventually be out of my golf game. On Sundays, Steve and our girlfriends would go try to do a dinner and a movie. Sunday's were Steve's only night off. There were also other benefits. We went to New Orleans for Saints games. My first football game was when Kyle Turley ripped off the helmet off the Jets player on a nationally televised game on ESPN. I had a blast at the game. The benefits were great. There was absolutely no downside to our friendship. He was a class act. In a sense Steve had become my Mr. Miyagi.

I told Steve about law school. He was very happy for me. Now with time passing real quickly, I needed to take care of my financial aid for Cooley. I filled out my application and sent it in. I was a nervous wreck. In case the reader has not noticed yet, I am a worrier. I waited my application results to come back. One month passed by and I had a response from the Cooley financial aid office. On the letter Cooley financial aid office basically told me that I could not get any federal financial aid due to being a none resident and a none U.S. citizen. I did not know what that meant but I had to find out. I went up to Dad and asked him. He had no response. All these years that I was pretending to be an American was catching up with me. The harsh reality of actually not being an American citizen presented itself to me for the first time in my adult life. It took me ten years to get rid of being Turkish. Now I had to start all over again.

I asked my father, "what do I do?"

Dad replied, "you have to apply for a permanent residency."

Dad said not to worry. I started feeling great about the whole situation again. All I had to do was apply for permanent residency. Once I did that, I would be able to get the federal loans that I needed. It would enable me to become the lawyer that I always wanted to be. I knew one great thing would come out of this process. As soon as I would receive my permanent residency, I was going to apply for my American citizenship. I no longer wanted to pretend that I was an American citizen. I was an American citizen at heart but now I wanted to become an American citizen on paper too.

There were financial problems that presented itself with this new problem. The whole permanent residency process was twenty five hundred dollars with an attorney. It was the twenty five hundred dollars that I did not have. I had to borrow some money. I knew my parents did not have it. I was on my own again. I had to ask Steve. I told Steve my problem. As a result he asked me how much I needed. I told him. He asked me, "when do you needed it by?" I told him, "as soon as possible." The next day he let me borrow the money that I needed. I was grateful. He said, "you could pay me whenever you have the money." I felt no pressure from Steve about his loan to me. I was just thankful that he would help me with my problem. My long battle with the United States Immigration Services was at its early stage. I could not foresee all the horrible things that were going to happen to my family.

10

One summer morning, I was sleeping in late. Somebody was beating on my door. I was really pissed off at this. Who the hell would beat on somebody's door that hard? I went downstairs with my boxers on. Opened the door. There were two people with wind-breakers on, right in front of me. One of these people was a man. He was about six foot two inches tall with blonde hair. He was very well build. I thought to myself, no way that I could take him in a physical confrontation. He had that look about him. You know that look a person has, that you automatically get irritated by. This person had that look. I immediately disliked him. The other person was a short stocky black woman. She had glasses on and looked nerdy. For some reason, I did not like her either. I asked him, "how can I help you?" The guy just glared at me. He said, "we are from the Immigration Naturalization Service." I was still sleepy. First thing that I could think about was that the I.N.S. was hand delivering my permanent residency papers. But that was not the case. This is how the conversation went on;

> I.N.S. agent sternly, "are you the only one at home?"
>
> I was shocked, "no, my little brother Bulut is sleeping upstairs."
>
> I.N.S. agent again angrily, "can I see your immigration papers?"
>
> I said to him, "is this a prank?" I was in a state of disbelief.
>
> I.N.S. agent showed his frustration, "no, this is not a prank. Can I see your papers?"
>
> I said to him, "I applied to for my permanent residency but I have not received any of my paper work back yet."
>
> I.N.S. agent raised his voice; "can I see your receipts?"
>
> I just smiled at him and said, "sure." Smiling at him made him get more agitated with me.

He looked at my papers and gave them back to me. He did not say a word. He was looking around the house to see if he could find anybody else. He was acting like there were people hiding inside the apartment. Like we would I hide what a joke! Did he honestly know what he was getting himself and his partner into?

> I.N.S. agent rudely asked looking around the house, "where is everybody else?"
>
> I told him, "tennis match." Mom and dad were at my little sister Rain's tennis tournament.
>
> I told the agent, "I could go get them. They are only ten minutes away."
>
> I.N.S agent replied, "that is not necessary."

I was being very cooperative now. Before I could say anything else, in walked my father. He was just as surprised as I was. I assume dad seeing two government officials talking to his sons surprised him. Dad had this nervous smile on his face.

> I.N.S. agent turned to dad with a real mean voice; "can I see your papers?"

Off course my father did not have any papers like I did. Neither did my mom or my two brothers.

> Dad said to him kindly, "I am here in this country as a guest of the United States government under a NATO visa." The whole family showed him their military identification cards.
>
> Apparently this I.N.S. agent had a hard on for dad, "your NATO status has expired in 1994 when you retired."
>
> Dad said to him in a real kind tone, "no way sir. You are wrong." Dad was right.

But, how could he prove his point to this Nazi bastard?

> I.N.S. agent raised his voice a little bit louder like he was putting on a show, "I am going to arrest you and your family and take you to our New Orleans office."
>
> Dad asked him in amusement, "is that necessary? We are no criminals, we will follow you."
>
> I.N.S. agent did not waiver, "I will arrest you, but the rest of your family could follow us."

I went to the tennis courts as fast as I could. I picked up Rain and mom. Rain was in the middle of a tennis match. She was winning. I told mom what was happening and she could not believe her ears. Mom was in tears. We got to the apartment as the I.N.S. agents were leaving in their Suburban. Mom got out of the car in a fury, she walked up to the I.N.S. agent that was sitting in the driver's side and asked, "Do you know what you are doing?"

> I.N.S. agent more angrier now, "get back in your car miss, or I will handcuff you and put you back here with your husband."

> Mom said in a threatening, "I.N.S. will pay for this."

> I.N.S. agent turned to me and said, "you better put your mom in the car now or I will lock her up."

I calmed my mom down and told her to get in the car. We were in our car following the government issued black Chevy Suburban on I-10. I was escorting two illegal aliens, mom, Bulut and one American Rain to New Orleans' Immigration Naturalization Service Office. I felt like I was an undercover I.N.S. agent. I.N.S. agent Ozturk's job was to take the detainees to their proper location in order to start the appropriate paperwork to get them out of this country.

The I.N.S. did not touch me, just because I had my receipts for my permanent residency application. What a crock of shit! I was part of this family too. I felt like an outsider again looking in. It was middle school all over again. The ride to New Orleans was a nerve wrecking experience. Mom had bunch of questions about the things that were happening. I try to comfort her, but it was hard. I had no answers for her questions. I was not capable of answering anything. The mental picture of dad being handcuffed was just enough to make me go crazy. But I had to be tough. Do you remember the flag that I was telling you about earlier? Well by the time, we were passing by Slidell, seeing that flag made me very sad. I was crying quietly inside. I saw the flag and I knew four members of my family were under the Immigration Naturalization Service custody for the next several hours. It was the longest ride of my life. But the flag represented people like my family. I knew we would get through this mess and there would be a lot's of questions that would be answered.

After the arrest, next several weeks' at home were very tense. One day, I got up early in the morning; I washed my face, brushed my teeth and came downstairs to write. Before I could sit down in front of the computer, I received a verbal beating by my mom.

> Mother in a real bad mood, "Umut, you better get your responsibilities straight, you have not paid any of your bills this month. If you don't like it here, you should leave."

I was getting the third degree. I did not even do anything to her in this particular instance. I just looked at her and stared at empty space. I thought to myself most of the time she wakes up from the wrong side of the bed. Whenever this occurs, I wound not even respond to her tongue-lashing. I would make an attempt to let it slide off my back. I would act like she did not bother me. I would just sit there and smile. I think that she thinks, just because I am the oldest that I owe her something. I don't care about any bills. I should not be paying for them. After giving every penny for years, I don't know what else to do. I know I do owe her for a lot of things. She carried me in her womb and nurtured me for as long as I could remember. I am thankful that she gave me birth and raised me over the years with tons of love. However at some point I can not take it anymore. I just want to scream from top of lungs, "leave me the fuck alone!" I don't mind working for free and giving all my money to the house. I only have a problem with one thing now and that is that I can not stand the tongue lashing anymore. In the past I would say, "okay whatever." Now it bothers me. If I could move away from home, I would. I can't just get up and move in the middle of this mess. I would have no place to go. Even if I did, I could not leave my family. I just couldn't. That is not how I was raised. My uncles took care of my grandmother for a long time. However I know trying to leave home does not mean that I do not love my family. It is just part of life. I grew up. It gets to a certain point that independence means more than anything else, that is why I wanted to go to law school. With law school, mother would understand that I was leaving for school. This would not hurt her feelings. It would only make her happy that her son is trying to be more educated.

I hope the reader does not mind me venting. Things were very tough at home. I have to let it out of my system. If I don't write about it, I would probably regret what I would say to her. If she knew how I felt, her little heart would be shattered. The play must go on and the actors must act. Since I am one of the leading actors here, I can not leave in the middle of the play. I must stick it out. These were crucial times now. However no matter how tough things got at home, life had to continue. Steve would always say the same thing to me, "ten years from now these would be the best days of your life." I would just laugh at him. I thought he was crazy. One day he said, "I would do anything to have my parents' back alive again. I would trade places with you in a second. Turk, time will take care everything. When these immigration problems are over, something else will replace it. So enjoy each day, because it goes by in a blink of an eye." I thought about what he said and dismissed it that afternoon. I said to myself, "what does he know?"

11

We moved into our apartment in the fall of 1992. When we first moved to the apartment, it was beautiful. We had tennis courts, swimming pool and a basketball court. It was a gorgeous place. To all of us including my mother it was a good place to live. The apartment was located in west Biloxi. We lived right across from the Broadwater Golf Club. I loved our location. We were close to everything. The mall was three miles away. The high school was five miles away. Kessler was four miles away. Everything that mattered to a growing boy was very near our apartment. If my brothers and I wanted to go anywhere, we would use our bicycles. My brothers and I were in paradise. After a month or two at the apartments we started making friends with our neighbors. The tenants at the apartment were mostly military people like us.

As the years went by like everything else in life, apartment occupants started to change. The ownership was changing hands. We were getting a new management in every several months. With changes new things started presenting itself. Our apartment went from military people to bunch of gang banger's and trailer trashes. It was a mess. For example; from 1992 to 1998 we had no cars in our apartment with flat tires. From 1998 to present, the apartment was full of ugly cars with at least dozen flat tires. The income base of the tenants went from middle class to no class in a short period of time. Our status remained the same however everybody else's status around us had changed drastically. The police started presenting itself in the apartment at least three to four times a night. The apartment had officially became the ghetto.

You would think the owners of the ghetto would change things for the better. That was not the case. The basketball court was thrashed. It did not get fixed. The pool went from being blue to green. Apartment did not fix it. The playground was full of beer cans and garbage. Nobody cleaned the playground. It seemed like the apartment owners were happy with the status quo. The ghetto was dirty. The garbage was not being picked up and the employees at the apartment did not care about this matter. People's animals were using the restroom in the middle of the sidewalk. Nobody would pick up after their animal's mess. This really got dad very angry. He started writing complaint letters to the management. It was absolutely to no avail. Apartment did not care. My father started complaining to the Biloxi Housing Authority. Their response in lay mans terms, "if things are that bad move out." I wish we could have, but we couldn't financially afford to move. Housing authority informed us that the apartment had become Section 8. To my understanding section 8 meant that the government paid most of the qualified tenants rents. These were tenants that could not afford to pay their own rent. If you could do the math, apartment management was brilliant in their business skills. The management got the apartment to go from okay to horrible, this only meant the paying tenants would move out. That led to new things. The poor people moved in. Not that there were anything wrong with being poor. We were poor. It was people that were less fortunate than we were that started living in the apartment. The apartment got as many qualified section 8 tenants as possible. Eventually this let to guarantee rent from the government. It was not like having military people for six months and moving. It was having poor people with no direction in life to move in and let them live at the apartment as long as they liked. They had year leases. Therefore, the government would pay there rent and the apartment would make lots of money with less help and less effort. Why the less effort? Do you think the tenants that are section 8 would ever complain about the environment that they live in? Hell no! They were just happy to have a roof over their heads and the apartment knew this.

In the fall of 2001 my father stopped paying rent. We did not pay rent in September, October, and November. For three months the apartment did not know what hit them. However, in December the apartment responded by taking us to court. The court proceeding did not go too smooth for us at all. The apartment had its lawyers and we did not. Dad was representing himself. The judge heard both sides of the argument and quickly came to a decision.

> Judge said to my father, "if you don't pay the fifteen hundred dollars by the morning you will be evicted."
>
> Judge turned to the apartment manager and said, "you people better clean up your act."

We had lost. Losing was not that bad. However, not having the fifteen hundred dollars was horrible. In less than fifteen hours, we would be kicked out of our apartment. My parents did not want to ask anybody for help. So, the whole think fell on my shoulders. I had to find fifteen hundred dollars by the morning. That night I went to work. I was in bad shape. I hated my life and my parents. It was my parents' fault for bringing me into this world. I went to Steve's office. I told him what transpired at court. He was in disbelief. I told him, I needed to borrow fifteen hundred dollars before the night was over. Let me tell you something about Steve. Steve is a hard worker. He is not rich. His mom passed away six months earlier and she left him some money. By this time I had already borrowed money for my permanent residency from him and now I had to ask again. It was a hard thing to do. But my friend Steve made it easy for me. He gave me the money without hesitating. I did not know what to say or do. I thanked him and walked out of the room with my pride gone. I could not let anybody see me crying. That included mother, father and Steve. The next day we paid the rent. We continued living at the ghetto.

The apartment manager that took us to court was a woman. Her name is Monica. Monica was about thirty-five years old. She had short curly hair probably at the time weighed about one hundred and forty pounds. She was definitely not ugly. But at the same time, she was not pretty. Before Monica took us to court she had started becoming friends with mom. Mom could not stand her but she had to act cordial. Monica kept trying to talk to us and find out more about our status. Monica told mom, "if you ever need help immigration help, I have an ex-boy friend in I.N.S. that could help you." Mom smiled and thanked her. Mom being the naive woman that she is told her about our status. Mom got in detail about my father's NATO status and ours. Monica was very sharp. She knew we would not move out. She also knew she could not kick us out. Now, she had to take the matters into her own hands. Monica got all this information from mom. Now these were her next several steps. First, she called the Federal Bureau of Investigations on my family. There she told the FBI about this unemployed Turkish man. She claimed to not know what he did for a living. Since these things were happening after 9-11 everybody was very cautious. However, FBI knew who my dad was. My father was always in constant contact with them over the years. Letting FBI know about certain business aspirations he had. In just a couple of years, he had an acquaintance in FBI's Gulfport field office. This information went to my father's acquaintance. He told Monica, "We are aware of this persons existence in Biloxi. He does not posses any harm or danger to anyone." Obviously Monica was unhappy with these news. Monica was a plain white trash. Not that I have anything against white thrash. Who knows, maybe I was white thrash? Monica had been married three times and had kids from three different husbands. She could not keep a man to save her life. Her kids used drugs and consistently got in trouble with the law. Mom always thought Monica was jealous of our family structure. Monica even told mom, "I want my kids to be like yours. How did you raise them so well?" Since FBI could not help Monica with this problem, she had to take it further. Her ego was hurt. She had received a tongue lashing by the judge months earlier in front of her boss. This was a woman on a mission. Monica got in touch with her I.N.S. agent ex-boy friend. He did a background check on dad and saw that he was not a permanent resident. He also saw on his computer screen no VISA date. From this point on he turned to his immediate supervisor and told him about us. How do I know all this? Court documents. This INS agent is a field operative. This is the lowest man in the chain of command. His immediate supervisor probably told him to go look into it. The supervisor probably did this in order to get rid of this ambitious field operative. The field operative's goal was simple. Arrest a colonel, bring him in, and get recognition. If you think I am full of it, listen to this, as he put my father in a holding cell at immigration office on the day of my families arrest, he got several of his buddies in there and told them, "look I have just brought in a Turkish Colonel." Think about that! Just like when I catch a big fish on a fishing trip, I brag about the size of the fish to my friends. There was no difference between catching a big fish and catching a Colonel.

Once Monica told her agent boy friend about us. He started coming to the apartment with his female partner. They started scooping us out. I saw him a couple of times and said "hello." Even when I said hello to him, I knew I did not like him. He had an ambitious look in his eyes even than. The day the family was arrested, we were (mom, Bulut, Rain and I) at the I.N.S. office for about five hours. Nobody would give us an answer. I was looking for dad. Two hours went by and a different I.N.S. agent came by and said, "your father will be with you shortly." I was relieved. For the first hour my father was in a holding cell. He was part of the puppet show that the United States I.N.S. was throwing on his behalf. After a year had passed by Dad told me what happened in that long two hours. While Dad was in his jail cell, Monica's boyfriend was showing off his marlin to all his buddies. Dad asked to use the restroom. He denied my father and said, "hold tight Colonel." As the puppet show continued my father said to me that, he accidentally did number two on himself. Dad said he was scared and he could not longer hold it. As he was telling me this, I felt the rage building inside of me. I wanted to run into a wall. I wish he would have never told me this. I went into total self-destruction path. I got off from work at twelve that night. I went to Steve's office and gave him my car keys. My next step I called Brian and told him, "be here to pick me up in forty-five minutes." I had three martinis in the next forty-five minutes. First time in my life I tried to forget who I was with foreign substances. Brian had to carry me out of the restaurant.

When dad came out of his jail cell into our holding room, he was pale. It had been two long hours since I was in this nasty building. I wanted to leave as soon as possible. This place made me hate America. I.N.S. agents were courteous enough to take of his handcuffs in front of his family. Monica's boy friend did his deportation paperwork on my family. It took him four hours. His supervisor told him to let us go at the end of the day. We did not even need a bondsman. We were just let go once the deportation paper work was done. They knew they had nothing on us. But as everybody knows, our judicial system is very slow. It would take a long time before we had to appear in court. Monica's ambition to get rid of us was beginning to look successful.

NOT PAYING RENT+ MONICA + INS AGENT Ex-boy friend = DEPORTATION

This was the equation. As I learned over the years every action has an equal possible reaction. Our life is full of small and big decisions. Those tiny decisions' eventually leads us to bigger decisions. Even as I proofread this now, it still does not sound that simple. But if you think about it, it is that simple. Now we were ready to move out of Fairway View Apartment's but it was a little too late. Isn't that ironic? Now looking back I liked to think that we had no regrets. We only lived one time. We tried to seize the day. These were the hands that we were dealt. We had to find an attorney. We were going into a war with I.N.S.

12

Growing up as a kid I did not have any bad habits. Even when I reached to my adolescent years I did not drink nor did any drugs. My absolute worst habit was either renting a movie or playing golf. I bought a lot of movies. By the time I reached to be twenty-one years old. I had over three hundred movies. I kept my life real simple. The simpler I kept it, the happier I was. At twenty-three years old I picked up my first bad habit. Since I never had any bad habits before, this was a big change for me. One day I got to restaurant a little early. Steve was in his office looking at the sports section real carefully. I wanted to know what he was examining the paper for.

I asked him, "Are you studying the sports section?"

Steve with a wise guy attitude, "no!"

I asked him again, "do you have a test on the sports page tomorrow?"

Steve again with the same tone, "no asshole. I am looking at the odds for this weekends football games."

I said, "for what?"

Steve again with his mobster tone, "asshole, I am trying to find out, who I should bet on?"

Since I did not know anything about the odds, I had many questions. He explained to me how the odds worked. He explained to me, if a team is favored by so many point's, it has to cover the spread in order for him to win some money. It was vice versa, if you bet on the underdog, the underdog has to loose by less than so many points in order for him to win. I was catching on, but I was very slow. It took me at least an hour to understand the rules.

My past history on sports betting was terrible. The terrible thing was that I had no past. I never gambled in sports period. So as any young dumb man would do, I decided to bet whenever Steve bet. I decided to pick four teams and decided to bet. I was going to pick four professional football teams. The way it worked was real easy. If you put twenty dollars on a four-team bet, you get back four hundred dollars. In order for me to win, my teams had to cover the spread. Not knowing what I was doing on my first sports betting experience I came out of it with four hundred dollars. All four of my teams covered. I was the next Kenny Rogers. At the same time like everyone else, I was trying to figure out, how to make more money out of betting. Now, I had credit with the bookie, I was betting like crazy. At one point I was betting on every game. I figured the more I betted, the more money that I could make. In two weeks I made more money in gambling than I did in the past month working. I was up and I was quickly down. Winning in sports betting is a real rush. Losing is also a rush. It made games more fun. I never liked losing. Who likes losing? I sure hated losing in anything in my life. I could be playing a video game and I hated losing on it. If I were not good at what I did, then I would just not do that again. Like I said earlier, I kept my life simple. In the next several months I started losing on every bet I was putting in. I was real unlucky. It was not fun for me anymore. In a span of five months, I won some and lost lots of times. I decided it was time to give it up. On December 23 of 2001, the day before my 24th birthday, I put my last bet in. It was a sure winner. Is there such a thing? Lakers versus the Grizlies, Lakers were a nine-point favor in Memphis. They had to win by ten points in order for me to collect two hundred dollars. Once the bet was in, I did not care whether I won or not. I knew I was quitting on my birthday. That night the Memphis Grizzlies won in overtime by ten points against the world champion Lakers. It was a sign. The next day I quit gambling for good. I did not need gambling in my life. Gambling made me very angry. I felt like I had no control over anything. Let me tell you a little secret about myself, I am a control freak. I must have a routine and with gambling I did not have that routine.

> Steve with an inquiring mind, "Turk are you betting today?"
>
> I responded with a sheepish grin, "Steve I am done gambling."
>
> Steve laughing now, "yeah right."
>
> I said, "I am serious."
>
> Steve still laughing, "whatever you say loser!"

That is how it ended for me. The next day without any hesitation, I gave up gambling. Now I look back and I am real happy that I gambled. I had to get it out of my system. It was a learning experience for me. However, I would never encourage anyone to gamble. I never gambled again. Not even at a casino. It is an awful way of throwing money away. Sooner or later, the house wins it all back. I know Steve did not gamble anymore either. Even if he did, I don't think he would have told me. He did not want me to start gambling again.

13

In July of 1990, Ozturk family was getting ready to move to America. My family consists of, dad, mom, Kanat and Bulut. We also had other Ozturk's moving with us to America. From my fathers' side of the family my grandmother and my uncle Saffet. Saffet was my fathers' youngest brother. Saffet lived in Alanya with my grandmother. He took care of her. Since he was single, that meant he had no attachments. He would be able to make the trip with us. Since his mother was coming to America, dad wanted Saffet to be with us too. Dad was looking at the bigger picture. Dad's plans were to move the whole family to America in the next two years. My other uncle Talat was older than Saffet. But he was younger than my father was. He would join us a year later in Biloxi. As dad received his work orders from Turkish Air Force to come to America, his vision was very similar to those settlers that initially moved to this great country of ours. He was searching for better life for his family.

Our journey began in August of 1990. Our departure was from Ankara. We flew for three or four hours to Paris in business class. Flying business class came to our way by total serendipity. When we bought the tickets from a travel agent we paid coach prices for our tickets and got to fly in business class. Travel agent decided to hook us up. This was my first trip in an airplane and I was impressed. Once we got to Paris, it was a total shock. We caught one of those van taxi' to our hotel, Le Meridianne. This place was a four star hotel in my mind. That night all of us were exhausted. We all fell a sleep real easily. The next morning Kanat and I were playing with the small refrigerator in our room. Every chance we got, we opened the refrigerator and got some goodies out of it.

That same afternoon my family decided to tour Paris. There were seven of us wondering the streets of Paris. It was a weird feeling. French people looked like they were Turkish but they spoke a different language. It felt weird. We walked the streets like any other tourist that would visit Paris for the first time. We were looking at everyone and everything. We were trying to find Eiffel Tower. We eventually found it. Eiffel Tower is beautiful. I am scared of heights. I have always been afraid of heights all my life. I don't know why I am scared of heights. I am not scared of going into an airplane and looking down out of the window. But, I am scared of climbing a tree and looking down. I did not want to go up at

Eifell Tower that day. However, my mom told me this is probably your only chance to go up to this magnificent tower. She did not have to say anything else. I was convinced. I went into the elevator holding moms' hand.

Mother with a very reassuring motherly tone, "don't be scared Umut!"

I responded like a child would respond, "okay."

The ride up the tower was fascinating. The higher I got, the prettier the scenery became. It was lovely. Finally we got to the highest point at Eifell. I stopped, looked down and realized how high I was. I got a little dizzy. The soccer fields and the lake that seemed so big just moments ago were tiny now. I held onto my mom's hand tighter now. We were on our way down now. Going up and coming down from the tower was two different exhilarating experiences. As I got lower, I was able to appreciated life more. I was very happy about living my life on the ground level. When we finally got off the elevator, I kneeled and kissed the ground. It was an experience I would never forget. However, I don't think I would do it again. If I did, I would probably have to take my mom with me. That night we had a nice dinner at the hotel restaurant. After dinner Kanat, Bulut and I ran through the hotel like wild animals. We probably played hide and go seek for three hours. I swear, at some point or another we were at every floor of the hotel. As the game came to an end, we went to our rooms for a good night's rest. The next morning we checked out of our hotel. Do you remember the little refrigerator that I was telling you about? Well, that little refrigerator cost us over four hundred dollars in room charge. Every time, that Kanat or I pulled the door open and got a drink or a candy bar from it, it charged to our room. How could we know that? We were kids. Even though mom and dad told us not to touch anything, we did it anyway.

Dad pissed off now, "what were you thinking?"

Our response, "nothing."

Dad angrier to our stupid response, "do you know how much you cost us?"

Our response, "no!"

Dad even angrier now, "four hundred dollars."

We did not know what that meant. My brother and I did not know the value of dollar. We were punished for the rest of our trip. However, we did not care.

We were kids. We were about to fly too America. That was exciting. For the next several hours at Paris Airport, Kanat, Bulut and I goofed around like any other child would do. We were running around screaming and laughing. We got our second break at the airport. All the business class seats were full. Only available seats were in first class. Therefore the ticket attendant wanted to know if we would like to fly first class. My father asked, "do you want us to pay more money?" Their answer was no. Flying first class was wonderful. We had our own section in the plane for seven of us. We had our own flight attendant. He got us whatever we wanted. I thought if America was anything similar to this, I was ready for her.

My first contact with America came in August of 1990. I was at an airport in Chicago. Reading about America as a young kid made me infatuated with her. I knew Huck Finn. I had read about him. Now I was going to a place where I could pretend to be Mr. Finn. From the things I saw, I was already in love with America. The crazy thing was, I was only in the airport. Obviously as you can see, it does not take much for me to love anything. I have always worn my heart on my sleeves. I guess that personal trait of mine will lead to my eventual downfall. That same day we flew to Minneapolis, Minnesota from Chicago. I know the reader is wondering; "why Minnesota?" We had relatives their. My fathers' uncle and his family lived in Minneapolis. We had whole clan of Ozturk's in Minnesota. Even my great grand mother on my father's side lived in Minnesota with one of my grand mother's sisters. All of the Ozturk's lived side by side. They were neighbors.

Our first day in Minnesota was a family reunion. I saw all kind of relatives that I have never seen before. Uncle's, aunts', great uncles, great aunts, cousins and nieces. Let me tell you about some of these people. My great-grandmother was ninety-eight years old at the time. She was an old woman that got shorter over the years with age. She was tiny. My grandmother was overjoyed for seeing her mom for the first time in years. My great grand mother would see us and ask us, "are you Kemal's sons?" We would just nod. She was like a little kid that craved attention. Guess what, my brothers and I gave her all the attention she needed. We were mesmerized by this ladies ability to go on for so many years. She was the oldest person that we knew. She kept on hugging us. Then a couple of minutes would pass by and she would ask again, "are you Kemal's sons?" At the time we thought she was just joking with us. But eventually we were told she had some memory loss over the years. We did not care about her memory loss at all. To us, she was precious. She would hug us and we would hug her back.

My first day in America was also a nightmare. I could not keep my big mouth shut. In 1988 my grand father passed away. He was absolutely crazy about me. I was his first grand son. As I was growing up, he would show me all kind of tricks. Tricks like, sitting in the ocean without moving body parts and still be afloat. As a seven year old boy seeing this, made him a super hero in my eyes. My superman was my grand father. He came to visit us in Kutahya two days before he died. He stayed the night with us. Before he passed away, he took my brother and I to school. He told us, "I will see you in Alanya." That is where he lived. He lived on a gorgeous beach house their with his wife and his youngest son Saffet. Twenty years earlier my grand father retired and then moved to Alanya. He bought land in front of the beach and then build a house. During the summers, all of us would go to Alanya and stay there for vacation.

He brought us to school that day. Before he left, we kissed him and we hugged him. From Kutahya to Alanya is an eight-hour drive. We did not have a car. Neither did he, he traveled by bus. That night as I slept, I had a dream and in my dream my grand father had passed away. The next morning, I got up to go to school. I told mom about my dream. She just smiled and said, "your grandfather is not going to die for a long time." I was relieved to hear her say that. That afternoon when I came home, mom was crying. I did not have to ask what happened. I knew the man I loved was gone. I was in tears. My father and his father were very close. He was also my fathers' hero. Let me get back to how I screwed up things in Minneapolis now. That afternoon in Minneapolis during the reunion, my grand mom and I walked into my great uncles (my grand fathers' brother) house. This is how the conversation went,

> I said, "hello everyone."
>
> Everyone said, "hello, you have grown so much."
>
> I smiled back and I said, "thank you."

Through the big crowd of family an older gentlemen emerged. I had never met him before. He came up to me and he kissed me on my cheeks and said hello. He resembled my grand father so much. As well as he should, he was my grand father's brother. Instantly, I liked him.

> My great uncle came up to me; "you must be Umut."
>
> I said, "yes."
>
> My great uncle, "how was your trip?"

I said, "great. We flew first class."

My great uncle, "how are you adjusting to the time change?"

I said to him, "I don't know." I did not even realize there was a time change.

My great uncle, "where is your grand father?"

I did not respond to that question for the time being. Everyone around me became silent. He repeated his question.

My great uncle, "where is your grand father?"

I looked puzzled and I finally responded "he is dead. He is been dead for two years."

My great uncle was puzzled. So was I. I told him he had been dead for two years now. My grand father had died of a heart attack. His eyes were full of tears now. Being only twelve at the time, I did not have the courage to stop the tears that were building in my own eyes. I knew what I had done. He was crying and I was crying too. It also did not help matters at all that I had never seen a grown man cry before either. It scared me. Everybody in the room with the exception of my grand mother was looking at me with hatred. At that second I again felt like a greaser at a social party. I realized no one had told this man that his brother had been dead for two years. What a group of hypocrites! Didn't they know my father would never leave his hero back in Turkey and only bring his mother. Did they think that they could hide it from my great uncle forever? I guess they did. I tell you what is sad; these are people between ages of twenty-five to sixty five years old. These mistakes should not have happened. They should have been truthful and told my great uncle the truth years earlier. Instead, nobody had the courage to say anything. Off course until yours truly accidentally told the truth. This was my first day in America. I was no longer flying first class in Air France. I was now grounded.

After several days in Minnesota, we were ready to fly again. Our destination was Biloxi, Mississippi. It was the home of Jefferson Davis. I was extremely excited about living in a place with such a history. Our plane did not come straight to Biloxi. Instead, we had to stop in Atlanta and take a smaller plane to Gulfport Biloxi International Airport. We arrived to Gulfport on a hot August afternoon. My father rented a car and we hit highway 49 south to the highway 90. At that point all I could see was the Gulf of Mexico. I had all the windows down. I was staring outside as my father drove. I knew that day this was a moment I would remember for the rest of my life.

14

803 Vandenberg was where we moved on base. All the officer's houses looked the same. I was wondering, why? My father told me, all the houses were the same because it was cheaper for the government. At the same time, the wives of the soldiers would not be jealous of each other's houses. Both of his reasons made sense to me. But the latter made more sense. Our house was huge. There were four bedrooms and two bathrooms. This was a palace for me. It was my palace.

My father started his job on base in late August. He was making sixty thousand dollars a year as a major. My uncle Saffet lived with us for the first month. In the second month, my father rented uncle Saffet his own place. A year later when my uncle Talat came to America he moved in with uncle Saffet. They were living at an apartment complex right outside of base. It was a gorgeous two-bedroom apartment. Off course, they did not have any transportation. My father went on and bought a car for them. It was a blue ford mustang. The car was awesome. Now my uncles had their own place and a car. In addition to these perks, they were getting a certain allowance from my father. Dad would never leave them without money. I know the reader is wondering, why? I will tell you, Turkish families are much tighter knit then your average American families. The oldest son is obligated to take care of his mom and his siblings. My father was doing an outstanding job as a great brother and a great son. In addition to these facts neither one of my uncles had a work permit to work in this country. This went on for two years. Mississippi was wonderful to us. We did get the royal treatment that I was expecting.

In 1992, a couple of months before we had to leave for Turkey, dad had to make a changes in his families life. At the beginning of the summer 1992, all of us went to Minneapolis to visit family. It had been two years since our last reunion. In Minnesota my father decided to buy a restaurant. It was a Turkish restaurant. My father's plans were this; my uncles would run the restaurant with my mother and they would be able to make a living. This was a solid plan. In addition to providing the family with a place to work, dad went on a little farther. He decided to buy a house. The house was worth one hundred thousand dollars. Dad applied for a loan and the house was given to us in less then a week. Now we had to worry about a restaurant and a house loan. Everything was good on paper.

Between the months of June and July of 1992, things went smooth in Minneapolis. The restaurant was making money. Everybody was working. Suddenly, as dad's tour of duty was coming to an end, the mumbling started to present itself. The voices began to bicker. Talat and Saffet were unhappy with the whole situation. It wasn't that they were working for free. Both of my uncles were getting paid well. My father always treated his brothers better then he treated us. My uncles were just spoiled. They were lazy. The past two years of vacationing did not help them either. That was my opinion. But that was not the case. They did not want to work for my mother.

Hell, they were not working for mom, they were working for themselves. It was for everybody's survival. As long as we had the restaurant, it was easier for all of them to get their green cards. That was dad's master plan. However, these grown ups were acting like children. The bickering eventually led to a big fight. My uncles and mom got into it. I must tell you, I love my mother. But she can get a little obnoxious. She is not an angel either.

>Mom being a bitch, "I can't work with bunch of lazy bums."

>Talat was angry; "you don't have to work with us."

>Mom, "you don't have to work with me."

>Talat, "why don't you go back to Turkey?"

>Mom, "you ungrateful asshole. I want you out of my house."

>Talat, "call your husband, see if I care!"

>Mom, "I will."

>Talat, "I can't believe I had to put up with your shit for two years."

>Mom in tears now, "wait till I talk to Kemal."

That argument was the final straw. My mother called my father crying. My father came back to Minneapolis from Biloxi. We had a family meeting. All the responsible parties were present. He tried to calm everybody down. It did not work. As a result of this fight and the inability of both sides not wanting to reconcile cost us a lot. We had to sell the house and the restaurant. We owned both of them for approximately two months. As a consequence, my father's credit was in pretty bad shape now. A week before dad had to go back to Turkey, mom, Kanat, Bulut, Rain and I had to make a trip back to Biloxi. I knew on that car ride back, that I would not see or hear from my uncles for a long time.

15

In Turkey majority of people are Muslims. Growing up religion was not an issue at my household. Both of my parents were descendants from different parts of the country. My mom's side of the family was from the more civilized parts of Turkey. She was from Istanbul. She was a city girl. In Istanbul people were more liberal in the ways that they perceived religion. However, in my father's neck of the woods, religion was more serious. Dad was a country boy. People in rural Sivas were more conservative than their larger city counterparts.

At nine years old, I began to realize religion around me. My friends were going to mosques with their fathers. Mosques were a place to worship for Muslims. Muslims worshiped to Allah and his profit Mohammed. I began to wonder when would I go? My inquisition on the matter only went that far. I had heard from friends that it was not fun. So I quit wanting to go. I thought it was a waste of time. Therefore, I did not ask dad about it anymore. I knew in my heart, that I was having more fun than my friends were. While they were at a mosque worshiping, I was running around the streets being a kid. I knew all my friends were envying me.

Once I came to the United States, I still did not have a religion. I was not a Muslim. I never practiced the religion. However people had a pre-conceived notion that if you are from Middle East then you are a Muslim. How could I be a Muslim?

Once I mastered the English language, there were always two questions that presented it self to me.

> People that I would meet always asked, "where are you from?"
>
> My response, "I am from Turkey."
>
> People, "what religion are you?"
>
> My response, "I am a Muslim."

It was too complicated to explain. How could I explain that my parents were free spirits? I thought for years, how could I be a Muslim? I did not know a single thing about the religion of Islam. I was lost. I did not have a religion. My crusade to find a religion began in high school. I started going to church with my friends. I had no idea on what I was looking for or whom I was going to find. My friends talked about church in a fun way, so I went. I was interested. People were so friendly their. My junior year in high school, I went to all kind of different churches. I was a visitor. I went to a Baptist church, Korean church and a Catholic Church. There was definitely more singing at a Baptist church. I liked that. My senior year in high school, I became the president of Fellow Christian Athletes. The funny thing was, I was not even a Christian. I guess since I went to church so much, everybody thought I was a Christian. As president of Fellow Christian Athletes, I had to began the meeting with a prayer. That was not a problem. By now, I was reading the bible and learning. I had knowledge about what I was doing. On one Friday night before a high school football game, I had to do a prayer through the public announcement system for the whole stadium. I was a little nervous. Everything went smooth. Everybody liked the prayer. I was real happy. My parents excepted me for who I was. I wondered later on, "why would they not except me?" My parents did not mind me going to church or being the president of Fellow Christian Athletes. They were always very open minded on my choices. They figured church could not hurt me. They thought church would only build me up and let me become a stronger person. I respected them for it.

During my first week at The University of Southern Mississippi, I became friends' with this guy from Tennessee. His name is Drew. Drew was a very friendly person. Drew and I liked the same things. We both liked play station games and sports. We started working out together at Payne Center. After a week of being friends, Drew had questions for me.

> Drew, "Turk, what religion are you?"
>
> I responded, "I don't know, I really don't have a certain religion."
>
> Drew, "Have you thought about Christianity?"
>
> I said, "yeah buddy I thought about it."

I went on and told Drew about my experiences about Christianity in high school. He was listening to my experiences with his mouth open. He was impressed with how open minded my parents were. Needless to say Drew was a devout Christian.

> Drew, "do you want to try something different?"
>
> I said, "sure. What is it?"

Drew, "do you want to go to BSU with me?"

With hesitation, "BSU?"

Drew, "Baptist Student Union. It is a place where we worship. You will meet a lot of good people their. I think you should come."

I said, "sure, what do I wear?"

Drew, "anything you want."

The next day on a Wednesday, he and I went to BSU. BSU was giving free lunch that day. I swear there were over hundred people present in the building. They were all my age, with the exception of few people. Everybody had name tag's on. Everybody was very friendly. I met over fifty people that afternoon. I also met the minister that day. He was this chubby guy that smiled a lot. I was automatically drawn to him. As I mentioned earlier, I liked people that smiled a lot. He shook my hand. He had a great grip. For the next several months, I began to interact with people from BSU. I was surrounded by bunch of people my age that were like me. They did not drink nor did drugs. They were able to have fun without the presence of these things in their lives. They had no bad habits. They were nice people. I liked that a lot. It seemed like all of them stuck together. For example, in intramural sports, they all signed up together for one team. Since, I was an athlete I played with them. That year I represented BSU in flag football and sand volleyball. I had a blast. My junior year came to an end. Before I had to leave for the summer, I stopped by the BSU to say, "goodbye."

Minister, "Turk, do you have a church that you are going this summer?"

I responded, "no."

Minister, "I have several friends in Biloxi. My good friend is the Preacher at First Baptist Church of Biloxi."

I said, "where are they located?"

Minister, "very close to your house." He had done his homework.

I said, "I will go to First Baptist this summer."

The minister prayed for me and my summer began. On the second Sunday of my summer I went to First Baptist Church of Biloxi. BSU minister's friend was an older gentleman. He was a super friendly person.

Preacher, "So, you are Turk."

I said, "yes sir."

Preacher, "don't be shy, call me by my first name, John."

I said, "yes sir." I guess I was a little shy at that moment.

Preacher, "We have a youth program this summer that I want you to be a part of."

I responded, "sure."

I was excited. I thought if it was anything similar to BSU, I would have a good summer. Same structure that I had at BSU would present itself for the summer. I was very happy. The person that was in charge of the youth program was this young guy. His name was Ashley. Ashley had just graduated from Southern Mississippi. Class of 1999. The minister from the BSU had helped him to find this job. He and I connected.

I started going to First Baptist Church of Biloxi throughout that summer. That summer the youth group was taking a trip to Atlanta for a Braves game then to Tennessee for a white water rafting trip.

Ashley, "would you like to go with us on this trip?"

I said, "sure, I would like that."

Ashley, "I am glad that you are going."

I said, "thanks buddy."

The trip was wonderful. I made a lot of friends that summer. Towards the end of the summer I got baptized. Everybody at church was so excited for me. I thanked everybody for there friendship and went home. A couple of weeks went by and I received my certification of baptism in the mail. I looked at it and smiled. I belonged to a certain group now. I had found myself a religion.

16

Biloxi to Hattiesburg is less than an hour away. During the school year of 1998-1999 I would always come home on the weekends. I had a second job in Biloxi as a valet at Treasure Bay Casino Resort. Therefore I had an obligation to come home and work on the weekends. Even though I was at Southern, I still had to make money and support my family. I also hate to admit this, but I would actually miss home. The whole school year I had the same routine. Monday through Friday, I would be in Hattiesburg. On Friday afternoon, I would head back to the coast. I had a beautiful car. It was the same hoopti that my parents drove years earlier, the infamous blue escort. The car did not look much. However, it would get the job done. During my junior year all I wanted from my car was to bring me from point (a) to point (b), then back from point (b) to point (a). Point (a) was Hattiesburg and point (b) was Biloxi. Blue escort would accomplish this task.

During the last week of my junior year, I left home late on Sunday evening to get back to Hattiesburg. It was about nine o'clock and unusually dark for an August night. Driving on H-49 is always fun during the day. But at night, it gets a little creepy. I hate admit I am a little scared of the dark. Every so many miles at a time on H-49, there would be a gas station. After the gas station, it would become dark and soon darker. Then several miles later a new gas station light would pave the way back to light. This would continue for the duration of the trip back to Hattiesburg. Thirty minutes into my trip, I needed to use the restroom real bad. It was the old number one. I needed to pee. I told myself loudly, "Umut, hang in there. Only forty-five more minutes to go." I did not want to stop anywhere. The road was very scary. I decided I was not going to think about using the restroom for the rest of the trip. It was mind over matter. Another fifteen minutes went by. Now I really needed to stop. But I didn't. I was not going to stop no matter what. It was to damn dark. However, I had to pee and relieve myself. I looked around the car and found a large fast food cup. I lifted myself off the seat as I continued to drive. Slowly I unzipped my pants. I put the cup in between my legs. I lifted myself on the seat a little more and started to pee in this cup. Keep in mind, I was doing about sixty-five miles an hour. I continued on peeing. I quickly filled up the cup and I was done. I put the cup between my legs. Now my left hand was on the steering wheel and with my right hand I was zipping up my pants. After zipping up my pants, I removed the cup away from between my legs. Now my left hand was on the steering wheel, my right hand was holding on to the cup. I was very proud of my accomplishment. I thought to myself, how many people can do this without spilling anything on them selves? Off course the answer was none. I could not wait to see my roommates and tell them about this extra ordinary accomplishment of mine.

I had the cup in my right hand now for about ten minutes. I had to get rid of this cup full of urine. I put the cup back between my legs and rolled the window down with my left hand. Driving with my right hand, I picked up the cup slowly with my left hand. Still there was no spillage I was the man. Going sixty-five miles an hour, I carefully stuck the cup out of the window. At that moment I was not thinking. I was still marveling at my amazing skill. As soon as I stuck the cup out of the window, all hell broke loose. The wind had taken the urine out of the cup and directed to my face. Now I was screaming, "I got pee on me." I continued on repeating, "I got pee on me." I was also screaming other obscenities. "I can't believe this shit." "Fuck!", I was about to go crazy. The screaming would not help. No one could hear me. I pulled the cup back into the car. It was still half full. I found an old shirt and wiped my face with it. I was furious. However, I still would not pull over. This was only a little setback. I was determined not to stop. I would not let cup of pee defeat me. What can I say, I am a very stubborn person. Still going sixty-five miles an hour, I was able to dry myself. Needless to say I was still angry. I looked around the car and saw that half of cup of urine between my legs. At that second I went absolutely nuts. I was mad at the cup. I blame the whole incident on the cup. If the cup were not in the car, I would have never done something this silly. I picked up the cup with anger and decided to throw it out as far as I can. I went into my pitching motion and tossed it out of the window as hard as I could. All of the sudden I felt this wet sensation on my left side. I had the urine all over me again. In the previous five minutes of hysteria, I had rolled up the window. When I attempted to throw the cup out, it hit the rolled up window and spilled all over me. I thought to myself, "this is a sign from a higher source. Just pull over." I eventually pulled over. I was furious. I kept on screaming obscenities to the wilderness. But it was to no avail. Nobody would care. At that precise second, I realized I should have stopped the first chance that I had. Instead I was a being a macho man. I quit screaming and calmed down. I started laughing out loud for about ten minutes in the dark. I had lost my mind. Twenty minutes later, I was in Hattiesburg. Before I got out of my car, I made a pact with myself that I would never tell anyone about the flying urine on H-49.

17

Today is August 8, 2003. On August 7th, I received a phone call from my attorney's office. The secretary from the law office gave me an appointment time for the following morning at ten in New Orleans. My attorney wanted to see me. It had been at least nine months since I heard from him. Only other time that I would ever hear from him would be about money. I would receive monthly bills from his office. That was the only other time I would know he was still working on my case. The secretary told me the purpose of the meeting was to get me ready for the permanent residency interview on eighteenth of August.

That night I could not sleep. I tossed and turned in my bunk bed as the night went by. The following morning I got up at six thirty. I took a glimpse out of my window to see how the weather was. It was overcast. I went downstairs and told dad, "I am not going to New Orleans this early. The weather is bad." My father started sleeping downstairs in the couch about a year ago. He said it was more comfortable. However, I knew the truth. He could no longer tolerate my mother.

I felt sorry for my father. Here was a man that gave everything up for us. In return, me and everyone else in the house, treated him like dirt. His response to my lame excuse was quite simple; "Quit making an excuse." I was real mad at him. Plus he was very straight forward, and that bothered me. I must explain I have always been very grouchy in the mornings. I would not talk to anybody for a couple of hours after waking up. His comment did not make me happy. However, it woke me up. I took a shower and went to wake up my friend Brian. This was the same clumsy kid that I was talking about earlier. Brian was twenty years old now. He would stay in our apartment a couple of times a week. Nobody in the house would mind. He was family. Brian and I started off for our journey to New Orleans. We left Fairway View apartments and turned right into Pass Road. The morning traffic was slow. I guess my fellow coastian's have not been awakened on this summer morning. It was surprisingly pretty outside. The sun was out by seven thirty. By now Brian and I were fully awake and were listening to my favorite compact disc of all time Mr. Frank Sinatra's greatest hits. I swear I love that song "My way". I could listen to that song for hours. Coincidentally, Brian and I had the same taste in music, girls, food, and cars. We were very compatible. We drove on Pass Road all the way to Highway 49. Their we went south for a several miles and then got on the Interstate-10 West exit to New Orleans, LA. The weather now was splendid. With Mr. Sinatra on the background, I had life by the horns.

After driving for about twenty miles or so, we stopped at the Louisiana Tourist Information Center. It was eight-thirty now. My destination was Polymnia Street in downtown New Orleans. Law offices of Mr. John Jacobs were located at Polymnia. According to the directions at the information center, I needed to take St. Charles exit and take a right. That would lead me to Polymnia. By the time I left the information center, I was told that I should be there in thirty minutes. It took me close to an hour. Between the Superdome and some street name that I can not remember, I got lost. Brian Brazil also known as "Pathfinder" helped me find my way. For twenty-five minutes I did not listen to him. It was my ego taking over my brain. Here is how the conversation went,

Brian, "Take the first right."

I, "The lady said to take a left."

Brian, "Take a right."

I, "You are wrong, I am taking a left."

After several minutes of bickering, I was lost. Being the stubborn person that I am, I blamed the whole thing on Brian.

I said to him, "I told you that I should have taken that right turn."

Brian smiling, "No you did not"

I, "Yes I did. You need to get your hearing checked."

Brian, "You are an asshole."

With a smile I said, "okay."

We were both laughing now. At nine forty I was in the law offices of Attorney John Jacobs. This was one guy that I truly disliked. He was the same crook that made our lives a hell. In my opinion, "All lawyers are crooks and all crooks are lawyers." I was not going to be like him. I knew I was going to be different, but in my clients eyes I would still be stereotyped as a crook.

Office of John Jacobs Attorney at Law was a beautifully designed two-storied southern house. To me it seemed like an exact replica of the house from "Gone With The Wind." This house was gorgeous. I was speechless. It is very rare that I have nothing to say. But I could truly say this was one of those rare moments.

The more I looked around this marvelous architectural structure, the more I thought about Scarlet O'Hara. At any given moment I thought, Scarlet would come down from the stairs and jump into my arms. What can I say, I am a hopeless romantic. I was still in awe of the building. I turned to Brian and I knew he was admiring this spectacular house also. At the present time there were three other attorneys in this building. I gathered my thoughts and went up to the secretary. The secretary looked like a woman in her thirties, short but plumb. Her weight made her look older.

Secretary, "Can I help you?"

I said, "I have an appointment with Mr. Jacobs at ten."

Secretary, "he still has not made it in this morning however he is on his way. Can I get your name?"

I replied, "Umut Ozturk."

Secretary, "Please be seated Mr. Ozturk."

I sat down on a brown bench that seemed older than this house. The longer I set the more my butt cheeks hurt. This bench was very similar to those fast food restaurant benches. It was uncomfortable enough to make you want to get up and leave. I got up and started looking around the office. There were over six hundred books on the bookshelves. I decided to make small talk with the secretary. My attorney was late and I was bored. By now Brian was waiting outside in the car. I had no one to talk to.

Secretary smiling, "feel free to move around."

I smiled back at her, "thank you. How long has this house been here?"

Secretary, "Over a hundred years. Mr. Jacobs bought the place in 1988."

I said, "I love your ceilings. Especially how high they are."

Secretary, "I agree. You have a good taste."

I thought for a second maybe this woman was trying to flirt with me. Then I thought about it for a second more and thought she is just being friendly. I continued our conversation.

I said to her, "I also like the stairs."

Secretary, "I don't. The stairs are too steep for me to climb up on."

At this moment I kind of felt bad. I knew her weight was the reason she had difficulties climbing up. I did not know how to react to this comment. I wanted to ask her if there were an elevator present in the building. I thought surely not! Not in a house this old. I looked back at her and smiled. "How long have you worked here?" Still smiling the secretary said, "about ten years." With my luck the door opened and Mr. Jacobs entered the building. The crook had saved me. I had no idea on how to end my conversation with the secretary. In he walked and the conversation was over.

Mr. Jacobs, "How are you Mr. Ozturk?"

I responded, "I am fine, how are you?" Mr. Jacobs did not acknowledge the question.

Mr. Jacobs, "I am sorry I am late. Give me a couple of minutes and I will be with you." I did not respond. The score was even now.

Mr. Jacobs resembled the looks of Rick Moranis. Short with glasses. He seemed like a nice man. But I knew crooks and Mr. Jacobs was a crook with a Juris Doctoris. Absolutely, most dangerous kind of crook. By now it was ten forty five. He went into his office and called his secretary. I was told to come in.

Mr. Jacobs, "Your interview is on the 18th of August at two. We have to go over some things. You could get approved for your permanent residency right away. Or the interviewer will take your file and examine it for several months. At that point he will decide, if he should give you permanent residency or not. If you get denied for permanent residency, you might be put on the deportation process like the rest of your family."

I smiled but I was angry, "That is no problem at all. At least there will be some resolution to this mess. I could find out if I could go to law school or not. If so, I will be happy. If not, I will be sad. However, I will move on. Thank you for your help."

The whole time I was talking to this crook, he was looking onto my forms. Never once making eye contact with me. I was annoyed. He stopped and decided to ask several questions. Mr. Jacobs said these are the questions the interviewer will ask you.

Mr. Jacobs, "Is it true your father is named Mustafa Kemal Ozturk?"

My response, "Yes."

Mr. Jacobs, "Is it true your mother is named Fatma Bedia Ozturk?"

My response, "Yes."

Mr. Jacobs, "state your full name please."

I said, "Umut Ozturk."

Mr. Jacobs, "Were you born in Istanbul, Turkey?"

I said, "Yes."

Mr. Jacobs, "Did you enter to The United States in Chicago on 12th August 1990?"

I said, "Yes."

Mr. Jacobs, "Did you ever leave U.S.A between 1990 to now?"

I said, "No sir."

Mr. Jacobs was doing his regular routine. Scare the client, act like he is superior to his client and then comfort the client. He was very successful with scaring me. He continued asking me questions;

Mr. Jacobs, "Are you a Muslim?"

I said, "No sir."

Mr. Jacobs lifted his head and looked at me. He seemed quiet surprised now. He looked back on his files and asked again, "are you a Muslim?"

I looked at him and said, "No sir. I am not."

He had a concerned look on his face. This new development had shocked him. He looked at his file and found my certificate of baptism. His client was a Christian. This crook had not looked over my files one time in the past two years. He had no idea. I was pissed off. He knew I noticed this. Mr. Jacobs also knew I was an educated man. However, I did not want to let him know that I was angry. I continued on smiling and tried to make small talk. I knew, since we were in war with Iraq, a country where Americans and Christians are despised. Things in the religion world were a little touchy. In addition to this Turkey was a Muslim nation in the Middle East. Turkey was tolerant of Americans however not tolerant of Christianity. Mr. Jacobs knew this little fact. Deporting me back to Turkey would certainly cause physical and mental harm for me. Therefore he knew, I could get relief from the American government.

I said to Mr. Jacobs, "I am the only Christian in my family."

Mr. Jacobs more attentive now, "I am a catholic. What made you become a Baptist?"

I did not want to divulge too much, "my beliefs in college had changed. I just grew up"

Mr. Jacobs, "How so?"

By now I realized he was a religious men. The iron bars between the crook and I had been temporarily removed. Now they were replaced by curiosity on Mr. Jacobs part. I looked at him with utmost candor and said, "I found god." Which was true. These three words made him change his demeanor on his chair. This was a revelation for me. All of the sudden in the past thirty minutes Mr. Jacobs went from being very nonchalant towards me to being my best friend in the whole wide world.

Mr. Jacobs now, "are you a black sheep in your family?"

Without hesitation I replied, "yes but not to my immediate family. Several months ago my mother's aunt came down to Biloxi. Growing up I was her favorite. When my brother told her I was a Christian, she did not talk to me for a week. Off course by the time the week went by, she was ready to go back to Turkey. Her words to me were simple, "don't tell anybody that you are a Christian."

I just laughed inside and smiled at her. Funny thing is Mr. Jacobs, "I knew at that moment, my aunt would never speak to me again. That was the end of our relationship. My feelings were hurt but my pride was still intact."

I stood up from my uncomfortable chair and looked at Mr. Jacobs and said, "I know who I am. I know I am an American in my heart and in my mind and no one can take that away from. I love this country the way I love my mother."

For a second I hesitated. Mr. Jacobs realized my hesitation and with a warm smile said, "please continue Mr. Ozturk." Now with all the pride and dignity in the world I made my final statement to him. "I don't need no stinking paper to tell me that I am an American. If I am not an American, than who is?" Again with all the conviction in the world I repeated these five words, "I know who I am." The crook did not say anything for a second. Then put his right hand forward to shake my hand and said, "don't worry about anything. I will take care of your case."

We shook hands and I was ready to go back to Biloxi. As I opened the door to step outside, the plumb secretary was trying to catch me, "Mr. Ozturk, Mr. Ozturk!" I turned around and smiled. She said, "Mr. Jacobs needs you to bring your tax returns for the years of 2001 and 2002. In addition to that he needs a letter from your employer describing your good standing."

The ride back home was more of the same. More Mr. Sinatra and a little bit more of getting lost. The whole way I thought, "what a jerk? It should not matter what religion I am for him to pay attention to what I had to say." Instead of going east to Slidell, I continued west to Baton Rouge. Brian tried to tell me that I was heading toward the wrong direction but it was to no avail. I did not listen. I got home at four in the afternoon.

18

It is August 14, 2003. This morning I got up at ten thirty. As soon as I opened my eyes on this morning, I knew it was going to be a bad day. I do not know why. Every since the meeting with Mr. Jacobs, I have been real down. I have been feeling real depressed. It feels as if someone is stepping on my chest. I felt like I could not breathe for almost a week now. Since my meeting with Mr. Jacobs, in order to go to sleep at night I started drinking a glass of wine. In any other situation I would never drink wine. I hate the taste of it. However now it helped me to sleep. It felt good.

I started snapping on people around the house. Whomever that I have came in contact with were receiving a series of tongue-lashing from me. I could not help myself. I felt like that teenager again, the one with no English or with no friends. The world was coming down on me real fast and I did not know how to react. In my opinion the worst quality a person can have is self-pity. I was experiencing self-pity first hand. I hated what I had become. I became the person that I most despised. I had four days to the biggest event in my young life. I did not know how to react. I was scared. I had millions of questions in my mind. Will Mr. Jacobs screw me? Will the immigration interviewer like me? Why would he not like me? After all I was a likeable person. But would whether he likes me matter? Would I get denied? Would I get deported? Would I get granted permanent residency? Is law school still a possibility? Would I get approved right on the spot? If I did not get approved, can I ever go to law school? I did not have any answers to any of these questions. In the middle of all these questions, my home telephone began to ring. No one was at home. I did not want to answer it. I looked at the caller I.D., it was my buddy Steve. I decided to talk to him. I picked up the receiver; I said, "hey guy."

Steve could tell I was down, "what is wrong now?"

I responded, "nothing, Yankees got their ass kicked last night 12-0."

Steve a big Yankees fan, "your ass."

I responded with a grin, "I am serious. They are going to get their ass kicked again tonight."

Steve, "your ass."

I am a big Derek Jeter fan however since I know Steve likes the Yankees, I pretend to hate them. I get a good rise out of Steve. I said again, "yeah, they suck."

This time Steve responded, "how about your boy Tiger today?"

Today was the first day of the P.G.A Championship. My favorite athlete in the whole world just shot a four over seventy and was eight shots back when his day was over. Tiger Woods in my eyes is a golfing god.

Steve knowing this tries to push my buttons. I said calmly, "he will win it this week-end." I did not believe in what I said, but still said it.

Steve responded, "your ass."

I responded, "I will see you at work asshole."

Steve, "bye loser. Just be ready to get deported."

For about five minutes my problems had quickly disappeared. By the time the phone conversation with Steve was over the problems reappeared. I now began to count the minutes, hours than the days till 18 of August. In my mind that day would make or break me. No matter how dramatic that sounded that statement was true. 18th of August would have two certainties. One, with an approval, it would bring me one more step closer to an American citizenship which I so desperately coveted. Two, with disapproval, it would put me into a depression for the months to follow.

19

Growing up as a young boy I always did some stupid things. When I was thirteen years old, I decided to shave my head. At thirteen years of age a little boy is going through a lot of changes. I guess by shaving my head I was coping with change. My first summer in Keesler went by quick. But at the same time it was a slow summer. Last week of that summer several of us decided to camp out in a tent. We set our tent behind Daniel's house. Daniel lived on base. His house was a short walking distance from my house. We had all the camping equipment that was needed. In addition to this, we had our favorite items; chocolate, marshmallows and Doritos. After we ate we decided to get in our tent and go to sleep. There were four of us in a two-person tent. It was very crowded. My friends were Joey and Daniel. The other person was my brother Kanat. Joey was a blonde haired pimple faced little kid. He was taller than rest of us. He was cocky. His father was a non-commissioned officer. Daniel had brown hair, clear skin. He wore spectacles. Daniel's father was a Captain in the Air Force. However his father being a captain did not change the fact that he was a nerd. At the time my father was a Major in the Air Force.

The last week of the school year I ran into a little confrontation in our school bus. Since Daniel was a geek. Everybody would make fun of him on our way to school. One day when somebody was about to beat his ass, I stepped in and said to that bully, "if you are picking on him, you are picking on me." The bully responded, "this is not your problem." Now I was scared. My heart was beating real fast. I started to sweat. I tried to keep my composure and said, "he is my friend. If you pick on him one more time, I will break your nose." The bully just stared me down for a couple of seconds. For a thirteen-year old boy, those few seconds seemed like an eternity. Now I look back and smile. I know it was just a pissing contest. Who would back down first? It sure would not have been me. The bully turned around and went back to his seat. My job was done. I protected Daniel from the bully. I turned to Daniel and said, "you have to stand-up for yourself." He did not say anything. He just stared out of the window. The bully was Joey. From that day on we all became friends. It was real easy for all of us to be friends, because we all lived near each other on base. Joey was a smart-ass. Daniel was the complete opposite. Daniel never said more than a couple of words. Joey on the other hand was gregarious and always talking. I could never shut him up. Daniel and Kanat were good friends. They were both quiet, Joey was a good friend of mine. Our group was divided into clicks but for that one glorious summer night, we were all best of friends. As I stared out through the open space of the tent that night, I became very hungry. I wanted real food. No more junk food. Knowing that no one else was a sleep, I asked to the group, "is anybody hungry?"

Daniel, "yeah."

Kanat, "yes I am."

Joey, "hell yeah, but where are we going to eat?"

We all got out of the tent with our pajamas. We grabbed three bicycles. They belong to Daniel's parents and his little brother James. Kanat and Daniel rode one bicycle per person. By luck of the draw, Joey and I had to share the other bike. I was the peddler and Joey sat on the cross bar. After a while we would alternate. He would become the peddler and I would sit on the cross bar. After a while this got to be very tiring.

Joey, "this damn bar is hurting my ass."

I responded, "what can I do about it?"

Joey, "just stop the bike okay."

I said, "no problem."

As soon as I stopped the bike, Joey jumped out and ran towards a house that was on the side of the road. He went into the neighbor's yard and grabbed a bicycle and started riding it. He had just borrowed it without asking the owner. Hell, how could he have asked? It was eleven forty five at night now. We needed an extra bike. We would return it in a couple of hours. The owner would have no idea when the morning rolled around that the bike was ridden that night. I did not see any harm in taking this bike. Since we had four bikes now, we were riding in a faster pace. We started riding our bike out of Vandenberg. We were headed towards the student dormitories. At twelve thirty, we were at the dorms. There was Pizza man delivering pizza by one of the dorms.

Joey, "Umut, do you see the Pizza man."

I responded, "yeah."

Daniel, "what are you going to do?"

Joey, "I am going to get us some pizza."

Kanat, "quick thinking. Good job Joey."

Daniel, "hurry up!"

I did not know what to say. I guess I was encouraging him nonverbally. Joey slowly approached the vehicle. The vehicle was old. The making of it was a Toyota. It was red. It was a total hoopty. Joey kept on looking around more and more. He was scooping the place out. I felt like I was in a movie. The closer he got to the Toyota, the more paranoid all of us became.

Joey, "the windows are down."

Daniel, "so!"

Joey, "there is three boxes of pizza here."

Daniel, "take it."

Kanat, "I am hungry, hurry up!"

I was real paranoid now, "check if there is any pepperoni."

We were about to steal three boxes of pizza and all I could think about was, whether any of the boxes contained pepperoni pizza. Now looking back, I just laugh at how stupid of a question it was. I could not believe how easy this was going to be. All three of us started grinning. Joey reached in through the window and grabbed all three of the boxes. He jumped back on his bicycle and we started following him. We were pedaling as fast as we could. We rode to the baseball fields. The fields were located right behind the dorms. We found a hiding spot. We were under the bleachers now.

Joey, "I am the man."

Daniel, "thanks Joey, you are the man."

I agreed, "you are the man."

Kanat, "thanks for the pizza."

I said again, "what would we do without you Pizzaman?"

After fifteen minutes, we were done eating. Joey was our new hero. Now it was around twelve thirty in the morning. We were all ready to go back home. Our tent was waiting for us. I could not wait till tomorrow to tell my adventures to my friends. I was riding in front of the pack. I was their leader. I had given Joey his new nickname "Pizzaman." Daniel, Joey, and Kanat followed me. Out of nowhere, several base cops showed up. Their sirens were on. Since I was in my own little world daydreaming, I did not see nor hear the cops sneaking up on us. I did not know what to do. I went into my defense mechanism and started smiling. One cop was pointing his gun at me and said, "put your hands up skin head." We all had our hands up now. Gone was the smile off my face. It was replaced by total fear. We were all placed in the back seat of different police cars. We were being taken to the security police building on base. There we were all put in different holding cells. Suddenly, it occurred to me. I was a criminal. I started crying. I could not retain my composure. Realization of being a criminal made me become sadder. After thirty minutes in that cell, I was brought into the interrogation room. There were two big cops in the room. Cop number one was a big white guy. Cop number two was a big oriental looking fellow. I thought to myself that I was stuck in a bad action movie. I was real scared.

Cop number one, "what are you doing out this late?"

With tears in my eye, "I don't know."

Cop number two, "did you steal a bicycle?

I responded, "no sir." Technically I didn't. It was not me that had taken the bike.

Cop number one, "tell us the truth."

I said, "I am telling the truth."

Cop number two, "your friends already told us, it was you."

I was shocked, how could they snitch on me? They knew I did not steal the bike, "no they did not."

Cop number one, "yes they did."

I was crying more now, "I did not steal the bike nor the pizza."

Cop number two, "who did?"

Now I was crying a little bit louder, "Joey, Joey stole the bike and the pizza." I was crying louder, louder. Not because I was scared anymore, but because I had sold out my best friend.

Cop number one, "who is Joey?"

I responded, "the blonde headed guy."

Cop number two, "that is not his real name."

I was baffled, "what do you mean?"

Cop number two, "I thought he was your friend. You should know his name."

He was right. I did not know my best friend's real name. His first name was Joseph. None of us ever knew. We just called him by the name that he wanted us to. The interrogation lasted for about ten minutes. But to me, it seemed a lot longer. I cried and cried some more. I was afraid. I knew for sure that I was going to prison. I knew in my heart, that I would never make it in prison. I was too weak physically to protect myself in prison. At one thirty in the morning my father and Daniel's father showed up at the station. I had never been so happy seeing my father before. My father had come to rescue us. The drive home was the longest five minutes of my life. He was yelling and screaming at Kanat and I. I did not respond. We had no excuses. We were both crying. Needless to say, I did not sleep at all that night. In the next several days I founded out Dominos Pizza did not press charges nor did the owner of the bicycle. We had to pay for the pizza that we had taken. We were very lucky in that perspective. However I was grounded for two months. Not so lucky their. I never ever thought about stealing anything again. Years passed. Me, Joey and Daniel lost touch. We grew up together but at the same time, we grew apart.

20

I was running real fast. Brian was right behind me. I had already run for three blocks. I had to get to the immigration office building in New Orleans by two p.m. Glancing at my watch I realized it was one forty five now. I had two more blocks to go in the next fifteen minutes. Would I be late to the most important meeting in my life? Surely not! I started to breathing harder and harder. Now I was sweating like crazy. The bottom of the immigration letter stated in lay mans terms not to be late. If late the penalty would be harsh. The whole application process would begin all over again. I could not wait another two years. I was running faster and faster now. I had my sandals in my hand. I was running barefooted.

I arrived to New Orleans at eleven that morning. I was determined to be on time. Brian's mother requested that I stop at Aunt Sally's and buy her some pecans. I could not object to this request. She was a dear family friend. So I parked my car at the post office building and decided to walk to Café Du Monde. We would have beignets there. Afterwards we would walk to Aunt Sally's and purchase the pecans. The walk at first seemed like a short distance. But as we walked farther in that August heat, it became longer. After forty-five minutes of walking, we were at canal road. I stopped a policemen and asked, "do you know how much farther to Café Du Monde?" He did not want to respond. He was obviously agitated by my mere presence. He ignored me. I asked again, "do you know, how much farther to Café Du Monde officer?" Asking the question for the second time got his attention. He looked at me and said, "three more miles from here." Three more miles seemed as if it was from Biloxi to Hattiesburg. I was annoyed.

Brian, "Umut, we could turn around."

I responded, "Why would I turn around?"

Brian, "you seem angry."

He knew me well; "no I am not angry. We came this far, we will continue."

I saw a trolley at its stop. I ran to it. I got into it as fast as I can. Brian was trying to keep up. I walked to the back of the trolley and sat down. I knew the trolley would take us to Café Du Monde in no time. I was proud of my sudden decision. We were riding and looking around town like any other tourist. The trolley was getting the job done. The trolley continued several blocks and made a right turn. Brian and I did not recognize this new development. We continued people watching. After fifteen minutes we were passing by the immigration office. I turned to Brian, "dude, we are back to where we started." Brian, "don't worry about it! The trolley will make a full circle and bring us back." What did I know? It was my first time in a trolley. The trolley continued, stopped, then continued again. With each stop, picking up new riders. Twenty-five minutes later we were by the Audubon Zoo. The zoo's location was right across from Tulane University. It was 12:45 p.m. now. There was another trolley coming back towards us.

> I turned to Brian and said, "let's get out and catch that one. It will take us back."

> Brian, "okay."

We got out as fast as we can. We ran to the next trolley stop and got on the trolley that was heading back to the business district. It was 12:50 p.m. now. With my luck, the trolley was stopping every thirty yards for new riders. There would be no way I was going to make it on time. I decided to get out of the trolley and started running. I knew I could move quicker than the trolley.

At 1:57 p.m. I was at the eight floor of the federal building. With obvious sweat in my face, I walked in to the immigration office. I put my documents on a desk and waited for my turn. My attorney showed up a couple of minutes after me.

> Mr. Jacobs, "how are you?"

> I responded, "I am doing fine."

At five after two, we were called into the office. The office had a tape recorder and a camera to record the proceedings. The interviewer was a pretty older woman. She turned to me and said, "I have to swear you in."

> Interviewer, "do you swear to tell the truth nothing but to truth so help you god."

> I looked around, "yes I do."

Interviewer, "I have some questions for you. Is your name Umut Ozturk?"

I said, "yes."

Interview, "have you ever been part of the communist party?"

With a smile on my face, "no."

Interviewer, "have you ever participated in conspiracy against the United States?"

Again smiling, "no."

Interviewer, "have you ever been part of a white supremacist group?"

Smiling once again, "no."

She turned to my attorney and said, "we are done here. His finger print's has been expired. So we need new prints."

Mr. Jacobs, "do we have to schedule an another interview?"

Interviewer, "no, we are all done here."

I did not know what was going on. I shook her hand and left the room. I turned to my attorney and asked, "what just happened?" Mr. Jacobs, "you got your permanent residency. Now you have to wait for your green card in the mail. It will have your green card in there and congratulate you in becoming a permanent resident." I was ecstatic. The interview I was dreading for months had started and finished in less then five minutes. I was overwhelmed with emotion.

The ride back home was glorious one that afternoon. Whole bunch of weight had been lifted off my shoulders. I was going to wait another month for the mail. That was not hard. But now, I had to find a second job to save money. I needed the extra money to move to Lansing in order to start law school. It had been three years since I graduated, I was finally on my way to chase the American dream.

21

True story, three brothers are named John, James and Clint Johnson. Their ages are John twenty-five, James nineteen and Clinton seventeen. They look like they were triplets. The story goes something like this. All three of them are on a vacation in Las Vegas. John is the only one old enough to do anything in a casino. While they are in Vegas, James and Clinton decide to buy fake identification cards to get into a casino. However, since they are on a vacation in a place like Vegas, they have no idea on how to acquire a fake identification card. Coincidentally, John has exactly two other copies of his licenses for his brothers. It was his expired copies that he had kept. John tells his brothers of this little fact. James and Clinton are happy by this new development. Before they go to a casino, they decide to try out their new identification cards at a strip club. Their plan is real simple. Each of them starting with John would go inside with twenty-minute intervals. The mastermind behind this plan John goes in without a problem. Twenty minutes later James comes in to the strip club showing a copy of the license John had used earlier. He goes in without a problem. Another twenty minutes passes by, Clinton comes into the strip club. The security of the strip club does not catch on. All three of the brothers get lap dances. James and Clinton are proud of their older brother's plan. They get a little intoxicated and started getting loud. Security guards noticing this approached the Johnson brothers. He asks to see some identification. Without hesitation the Johnson brothers show their licenses. Security guard realizes that all of the identification cards belong to Mr. John Johnson. It has Mr. John Johnson's picture on all of them. Security guard does a quick double take at the pictures and the brothers. Security guard calls for a back up and escorts the infamous Johnson brothers out of the strip joint. I heard this story all the way through high school. It had become an urban legend at Biloxi High. It was every boy's dream to have fake identification cards to go into strip clubs back in the day.

This brings us to present day. One Saturday afternoon I was coming back from the West Biloxi Library. On my way home there is a car wash on the left side of the road. I see a friend of mines car at the car wash and decide to stop.

I, "hey Chris, what is going on?"

Chris, "nothing much. Did you hear I got into an accident?"

I said, "no buddy. I did not know."

Chris, "my truck got hit from the front. My parents will not get it fix, they are selling it."

I said, "I am sorry to hear that."

Chris, "what have you been doing?"

I responded, "I have been working. What have you been up to?"

Chris, "nothing much. I have been going to casinos and gambling."

I was a little surprised, "Chris, aren't you nineteen?"

Chris, "yeah but, I got a fake I.D. for twenty-five dollars."

Chris reaches into his valet and shows me the I.D. I look at the picture and it is his. I look at his information and smile. I realize that his last name is changed to something else. I am baffled to see how real his identification card looks.

I ask, "how did you get this?"

Chris, "Josh has been making these for forty dollars a pop."

I asked, "but, how?"

Chris, "he has the format on his computer. Pretty cool isn't it?"

I replied, "yeah, but he could get in a lot of trouble for this."

Chris, "I know."

Chris, Bulut and Brian were good friends. That same afternoon Bulut, Brian and myself were eating lunch in the mall. I saw three kids approaching our tables. One of them was Josh. I knew Josh since he was eleven. I coached him for several years. He was a fat kid as a youngster. But once he went through puberty he had shed all that weight. He was a babe magnet. He was the only child in his family. Usually only children with no siblings turn out to real spoiled. This was not the case with Josh. He was a great kid. His mother and father had done an excellent job with him.

Josh, "hey!"

I replied, "what's going on?"

Brian, "hey Josh."

Bulut, "what's up?"

Josh, "I just came to buy a couple of things for school."

Brian, "when do you leave?"

Josh, "Thursday."

Brian, "I need a favor before you leave."

Josh, "what is it?"

Brian, "you know."

Josh, "what?"

Brian did not want to talk about this delicate matter in front of Josh's friends.

Brian, "you know what I need."

I interrupted and said, "we heard that you were in business."

Josh smiling, "yeah. Just call me in an hour I will get you what you need."

Bulut, "thanks."

Brian, "thanks."

That night Brian and Bulut called Josh. Josh told the boys to bring an old license with them. After the phone conversation was over, Brian and Bulut approached me;

Brian, "we are going to Josh's', do you want to come with us?"

I said, "no thanks."

Bulut, "come on."

I reiterated, "no thank you."

Brian, "come on, it will be fun. You could see how he makes these fake i.d.s"

Brian had a good point. I was curious but replied, "no thanks."

Bulut again, "come on."

Brian in Turkish now, "come on Umut abi."

Bulut again, "lets go. He is waiting."

We got to Josh's house about nine forty five that night. Brian knocked on the door. Josh's mom answered the door and let us in.

Ms. Lydia, "hey guys, it has been a while."

We all replied, "yes ma'am."

Ms. Lydia, "Josh is in his room."

We all replied, "thanks."

We walked into Josh's room. His room was real nice, big room with the computer at one end and the television on the other. I thought for a second, this is the kind of room I would like to have some day. Josh was on the computer.

Josh, "hey Umut! I did not think you were coming."

I replied, "I wanted to see the master at work."

With a sheepish grin Josh replied, "thanks."

Josh looking at our future criminals and asked, "who wants to go first?"

Brian replied, "I'll go first."

Josh, "did you bring an old license?"

Brian, "yes." Brian handed the old license to Josh.

Josh took off the top layer of the license. He got sandpaper and started rubbing the sandpaper side to side, up and down until all the information was removed. The step number one was over.

Josh with a digital camera in his hand, "Brian stand against the wall, facing me."

Brian, "where?"

Josh, "anywhere you want?"

Brian, "here."

Josh, "sure."

Josh had taken Brian's picture. Now he downloaded the picture to his computer. On Josh's screen was the exact copy of the Mississippi license.

I asked Josh, "how did you get that on your screen?"

Josh, "I spend a lot of time on the computer. After a while, I was able to find anything I wanted."

I was pretty amazed at my young friend's talents. Josh played with the picture a little and put it over the license on the computer.

Josh, "what name do you want?"

Brian, "I don't know!"

Josh, "we will keep your first name and change your last."

Brian, "why do you want to keep my first name?"

Josh, "if security catches you at a casino and says your name, it will be easier for you to respond to the name that you are used to."

Brian, "that makes sense."

With a cocky grin in his face Josh replied, "I know."

Brian, "how about Brian Pitt?"

Bulut, "how about Brian Cruise?"

Brian, "how about Brian Gibson?"

Josh, "I am serious. Give me a good last name."

Bulut, "how about Hannibal Lecter?"

All of us in the room were laughing now. Brian decided he wanted a last name that was believable. After a while Josh got tired of waiting and gave him a last name on his own. He rearranged Brian's driver license number and his address. He made a laminated print out and put the information on top of the sanded card. The top part he had peeled off earlier was put back on top of the new information. He got an iron, put a cloth on top of the new license and ironed it. Brian had a fake I.D. now. Bulut went through the same process. With same redundant jokes, we left our friend's house at eleven thirty. Bulut and Brian were happy with their additional licenses. But at the same time, they were skeptical.

Bulut, "will it really work?"

Brian, "I don't know?"

Bulut turned to me; "will it work? What would happen if we get busted?"

I answered, "I don't know."

Brian and Bulut were anxious to try out their new toys. Before they tried the licenses, I instilled a little bit more fear into them. I told the boys about the Johnson brothers. I added new things here and there. Urban legend had to continue.

Bulut very interested now, "so what happened to them?"

I said, "they got kicked out of the strip club."

Brian, "not that, did they get in trouble?"

I said, "no, however they had their licenses picked up."

Brian, "that is no problem."

Bulut, "as long as they don't call the cops."

The next night we went to a casino. Those two went in before me. I went in about ten minutes after them. They were just looking around in awe of the place. Pretty cocktail waitresses were every where. These two just stared and stared some more. We left after ten minutes. They were happy that their fake i.d.s had worked. The cards were flawless. Bulut was Mr. Pacino and Brian was Mr. Brando. I am just joking about their last names.

22

I met Haruka in October 2002. Our introduction came through mutual friend named John Thomas. John Thomas played soccer for me during the 2002-2003 soccer year. He was an excellent soccer player. Fast and strong but lacked discipline. John Thomas and I played golf and kept in touch with each other after the season ended. We started becoming good friends, even though he was younger then me. In October, J.T. called me.

John, "what's up?"

I said, "nothing, what's up with you?"

John, "are you ready to meet the best player on the coast?"

I said, "okay, who is he?"

John, "Haruka. If you want him on the team, I will bring him to practice."

I said, "alright bring him."

Our second practice of the year, I met Haruka. Haruka was a Japanese exchange student that attended D'Iberville High School. At the initial meeting, he did not look much. Haruka was short. He was about 5'2 inches tall. But he was not skinny. He was built like a mini refrigerator. I immediately had taken liking to him. Towards the end of the previous season Haruka's twin brother Haruki played for me. I did not know his twin brother Haruka was about to come to this country a year after Haruki.

I said, "hello Haruki."

Haruka responded, "it is Haruka."

His accent made me smile "I am sorry Haruka. Would you like to play for us?"

Haruka, "yes."

The more he spoke the more I smiled. To me it was funny. I quietly wondered to myself; is this how I spoke when I first came to America? Was I this funny? Surely not! But than again only the people that knew me back then knew. Haruka started practicing with the rest of the team. He immediately showed he was the most skilled player on the team. The kids that played on Biloxi United played for me as kids. Back then they were eleven and twelve. Now they were eighteen and nineteen years old. My kids were good kids. They immediately welcomed Haruka to the team. He came to America in August and in October he had full team of friends.

In December, I took the team to Camp Wilkes. We were going to stay at a cabin their for two nights. It was going to be a team bonding experience. The twenty-third and twenty-fourth of December was our training camp. The evening of the twenty-third we moved into our cabin. My team was probably the most ethnically diverse team on the coast. I had kids from all over. Turkish, Peruvian, black, white, Japanese and kids from D'Iberville. We were deep in diversity. The cabin's name was Big Jo. Big Jo's cost was not much at all. It cost each kid ten dollars to stay their two nights. There were ten bunk beds all the way across the cabin. When we entered the cabin all my boys were surprised. They did not know what to expect. Everybody sprayed Lysol on their beds and put their bed covers on their beds. Haruka was totally lost now. Haruka, Bulut, Brian and J.T. were in charge of starting the cabin fire. It took them two hours. But they were successful. Those two days we played fox and manhunt. Hide and go seek and off course a little chess in the cabin. Needless to say, we stayed up real late both nights. At the end of our stay we had built a team. Haruka went from being very shy kid on the twenty-third day of December to being very talkative on the morning of the twenty-fifth of December. His grasp of the English language was suspect. But he was trying hard. We did not care whether he spoke well or not. We were his family for the next seven months.

By February, the language barrier had been removed. Haruka was making progress in a rapid pace. He was absolutely the best player in our league. He was becoming real popular around the coast. In April of 2003, Haruka led us to the district finals. Haruka became a good friend of mine during the process. He did not say much to me. But I talked to him whenever I could. I wanted to know about his family and his culture. Initially because of his cultural background he was shy towards me. Once May rolled around, he realized he had no choice but to talk to me. That is my personality, even if a person does not like me, if I like him, I am going to continue on being his friend till the barrier is broken down.

However there are those people that I do not like from the beginning. Haruka was not one of those people.

In June, Haruka had one more month left in the United States. He would leave on July 9th. On June 25th and 26th our team was in Meridian, Mississippi competing in the state games of Mississippi. The whole team knew, this would be Haruka's last week with us. I was sad. I got used to this guy now he was going to leave. On the 26th of June, we played Southwest Jackson. That morning Southwest Jackson beat us 1-0. Towards the end of the game Haruka had missed a one on one with the goalie. He was devastated. In between games at the hotel, we all went swimming. I went to my room and brought this four feet tall trophy to the pool.

>I turned to Brian, "go get Haruka."

>Brian, "he is sad."

>I responded, "if you get him, he will be happy."

>Brian, "okay."

Five minutes later Haruka looking very disappointed showed up. All of his teammates were out of the pool now.

>I turned to Haruka and the team; "this trophy is being presented to the best player, friend and most of all to the best person on this team, Haruka Nishimura."

All of his teammates were clapping for him. Haruka walked towards me. He put his hand out to shake mine, instead he received a big bear hug. He picked up his trophy over his head and beamed like a true champion. We did not win any games that weekend. However, we made a lasting impression on each other's hearts.

July 9th 2003 was the day, my friend would leave America after one year of stay and go back to Japan. His plane would depart at five thirty in the morning form Biloxi-Gulfport International Airport. On our last night Brian, Haruka and I went to a seafood restaurant and had dinner. Haruka taught us how to say cheers in Japanese. Every time we had a drink we said, "Campai!" Haruka told us, he has to be at the airport at four-thirty in the morning. He had to call it a night. We told him we would be at the airport to send him off. He did not believe us. He did not think we would be able to get up that early. What he did not know was that neither Brian nor I planned to go to sleep that night. Guess what, Brian and I were at the airport that morning at four thirty. We were tired. We went up the escalator and saw our little friend sitting next to his host mom.

Haruka, "hello."

Brian, "hello."

I said, "hello."

Brian, "did you think we were going to be here?"

Haruka, "yes, I knew you would come. You would not disappoint me."

Brian, "no we wouldn't."

We sat there that morning and talked to Haruka for an hour. To me this was the first time in the past year that he looked like a tourist. When his flight number was called, he started crying. In return, Brian and I started getting emotional. I did not care. Crying was not a bad thing.

Brian, "I am going to miss you Haruka."

I added, "me too."

Haruka, "I am going to miss you guys too."

I said with a teary eye, "don't forget about us."

Haruka, "I won't."

Brian and I watched him walk down the stairs to his plane that morning. We were devastated. But at the same time we were happy for him. He was going back to be with his real family.

When I came home that morning I could not sleep. I went downstairs and got on one of my fathers web pages and wrote this article in tribute to my friend Haruka. I wanted every one of his friends and family to know that their son, friend, nephew, young Haruka left an imprint in our hearts that would last for an eternity. Once the article was over, I e-mailed Haruka and told him to check the website under the words writers column that same day.

NISHIMURA WINS MVP

Japanese exchange student Haruka Nishimura wins the prestigious Most Valuable Player trophy for his Mississippi soccer team. Haruka also was an All State soccer player for the state of Mississippi. He represented Biloxi in the State

Games of Mississippi in June 27-28 of 2003. In Meridian, Mississippi he helped his team win third place in the State Games. This is what one of his teammates Rickey had to say about young Haruka, "Haruka is the best soccer player that I have ever played with. But at the same time, he is the best person that I have ever met." Haruka played club soccer for Biloxi Soccer Organization for eight months. There he played twenty-five games for Umut Ozturk. He led Biloxi United in goals with twenty-seven and in assists with thirty-two.

Haruka led Biloxi United to the city championships. His highlight of his soccer season came in April 12-13 in Gulfport. In the Southern District Semifinals against Laurel, with the score tied at 1-1 Nishimura scored the goal of the year. Bulut Ozturk of the Biloxi United dribbled the ball down the left sideline and crossed the ball to the penalty spot, their Nishimura came out of nowhere with a diving header which hit the upper ninety. The crowd was going crazy. Haruka's teammate and good friend Danny said, "it was the greatest goal that I have ever seen. Haruka is a clutch player and he came out of nowhere. I am hoping that he will take us to the state championships." Brian Brazil of Biloxi United had a different take on Haruka's goal "Nakata will take us all the way."

Haruka left United States in July 9th. As a person writing about a dear friend, he was not only a great soccer player but also a great person. Coach Ozturk of Biloxi said this about young Japanese sensation, "he comes from a great family background and he is a very respectful young men. I wish him all the luck in the world."

23

Tonight is August 26, 2003. The most unusual thing happened at work this evening. Young Mexican friend of mine named Marco approached me and asked me;

>Marco, "what will happen to me if I get pulled over?"
>
>With a hesitation in my face, "what do you mean?"
>
>Marco, "you know, I have no papers."
>
>Knowing full well what he meant, "what do you mean?"

In the past several months Marco and I had become friends. Marco was a bus boy from Mexico. He was a nice guy. He did not like his job. One of our co-workers got Marco the job a couple of months earlier. He was also a Mexican. For some reason Marco could not stand him. Marco would not tell me the reasons. But I figured out on my own. Our mutual Mexican friend was a rich boy. He worked and spent his money on himself. There was nothing wrong with that. However Marco had girlfriend and a new baby girl. He supported his family. We talked at work a lot. We got used to each other and we confided to one another about our problems. When Marco started working, he had told everyone he was twenty-four years old. I did not buy it. After a while, he had told me he was only eighteen.

>Marco, "I have been on my own since fourteen years old. I crossed the border at a young age and never returned. I left my brothers and sisters in Mexico. I missed them."
>
>In admiration of my friend's courage, "is Marco your real name?"
>
>Marco, "yes."
>
>I asked, "how did you get papers?"
>
>Marco responded, "when I crossed the border to Texas, I met this guy. He helped me get a new birth certificate and a new identity."

I was speechless. Marco was similar to one of those characters out of a Grisham novel. I said, "but, how?"

Marco, "it cost me five-hundred dollars. With fresh papers, I have been on my own every since. What will happen if I get pulled over?"

I was knowledgeable about things like this, "the worst thing that could happen is, they will send you to New Orleans Immigration Office. Their, I.N.S. will do paperwork on you to begin the deportation process."

Apparently a little scared, Marco asked, "what do you mean?"

I responded, "you will be in the I.N.S. custody for a maybe seventy two hours the most and bail out. Then you would have to go through the I.N.S. deportation procedure."

Marco was shocked now. He looked at me and asked, "how do you know all this?"

True magician would never tell his tricks. Ask David Copperfield? I would never tell him my family's status. I was too embarrassed. However, I will make an exception here. When my family got arrested on August 21, 2002, there were some initial charges. The I.N.S. alleged that my father, mother, Kanat and Bulut;

> 1. You are not a citizen or national of the United States;
>
> 2. You are a native of Turkey and a citizen of Turkey;
>
> 3. You were admitted to the United States at Atlanta, Georgia on or about February 19, 1994 as a nonimmigrant N-1 with authorization to remain in the United States for a temporary period not to exceed December 31, 1999;
>
> 4. You remained in the United States beyond December 31, 1999 without authorization from the Immigration and Naturalization Service.
>
> On the basis of the foregoing, it is charged that you are subject to removal from the United States pursuant to the following provision(s) of Law:
>
> Section 237(a)(1)(B) of the Immigration Nationality Act(Act), as amended. In that after admission as a nonimmigrant under Section 101(a)(15) of the Act, "you have remained in the United States for a

time longer than permitted, in violation of this Act or any other law of the United States."

These were the charges. Charges one and two were correct. However, charges three and four were wrong. Responding to charge three; my family had arrived to the United States at Chicago in August of 1990. My families status is Nato-2. We were allowed to stay in this country until 2006 or duration of stay. Just on charge three alone, we had discovered three discrepancies. Now, responding to charge four; according to our I-94, which stated D/S; which mean duration of stay. At no point my family needed any other authorization from the I.N.S. In addition to these discrepancies, our address and phone numbers were wrong. According to file no:A95 605 732, our address and phone number was 2224 Pass Road and our phone number was 388-3741. Our address was correct on this form. However, our phone number was not. It was the number of our apartment manager Monica. This gentleman that had done all this paper work on us was Monica's lover.

My father had caught on to these discrepancies from the beginning. We knew these charges would not stand. Now we had to prove it. We needed to find a good attorney. Someone that was a fighter someone that would go blow to blow with the system. If not, my family would be divided into two. Pop, mom, Kanat, Bulut being deported. As a result this would leave Rain and I in this country. Our family would be divided forever.

24

During my crisis for law school in late 2001, I needed to find an attorney. I opened up the yellow pages. I looked under immigration attorneys and saw three names present. I dialed the first number I saw. It was the office of John Jacobs. I had spoken with Mr. Jacob's secretary and made an appointment. I met Mr. Jacobs and immediately I did not warm to him. For some reason I did not like him. However it did not matter. Any idiot could fill out my papers. Any idiot could get my case done for me. How could he not take it? Off course Mr. Jacobs took my case. I had to pay large sums of money that I had borrowed from Steve for this mess. I could have done this by myself. I despised that crook. Sometimes I think to myself, "what if I picked someone else? Would my case be done quicker?" August 21,2002 was the day Mr. I.N.S. agent came into my life. He and his partner were barking around my apartment.

I asked him "can I call my attorney?"

I.N.S. agent, "sure."

I dialed Mr. Jacobs' office. His secretary answered. I said, "hello this is Umut Ozturk, may I speak to Mr. Jacobs?"

Secretary, "Mr. Jacobs is with a client. Can I take a message?"

I responded with total disgust, "no you may not. Now listen to me carefully, I have two I.N.S. agents in my apartment, I need to talk to Mr. Jacobs."

Secretary realizing the importance of my call, "one second."

About a minute passed by, Mr. Jacobs was on the phone. Mr. Jacobs, "hello Mr. Ozturk. How can I help you?" His voice was unfriendly as ever.

I responded, "there are two I.N.S. agents looking for my family. What should I do?"

Mr. Jacobs, "put one of the agents on the phone."

I handed the phone to lover boy, "hello." They spoke for several minutes.

Apparently they were friends. Lover boy turned my way and said, "he wants to speak to you."

I said, "hello."

Mr. Jacobs, "this gentlemen is going to take your family to New Orleans. There, he has to make your family go through some paperwork. Now it is going to be okay. I will make an appointment for tomorrow, in order to discuss this matter farther."

I did not trust this crook. I thanked him and I hung up. This was the way Mr. Jacobs became the family attorney. It was just an occurrence of bad luck or lack of options. Yellow pages had failed me.

25

My family had received a letter from the deputy assistant district director of investigation in September of 2002. Our first appearance in court was scheduled for December 2002. This is what the letter stated;

YOU ARE ORDERED to appear before an immigration judge of the United States Department of Justice at: The Immigration Court, 1 Canal Pl., 364 Canal St., Suite 2450, New Orleans LA 70130.

My father would meet with Mr. Jacobs on several occasions between August to December.

> After the first meeting, I asked my father, "how do you like our attorney?"
>
> Dad looked at me with disgust and said, "he is a piece of shit."
>
> I was not surprised to this at all. I asked, "why?"
>
> Dad looked and said, "he is an ambulance chaser. He does not care whether he wins our case or not. All Mr. Jacobs cares about is the five grand he is going to get from us between now and our first court appearance."
>
> I asked, "why do you say that?"
>
> Dad looking more tired now, "son, I took all the necessary paperwork to him and he still was trying to beat around the bush. I took him the laws that I have found. On these laws, it clearly states our immunity from the I.N.S.. Needless to say, he was irritated by my own research."
>
> I was in disbelief now, "but, but, dad, I think you are exaggerating. You are probably analyzing Mr. Jacobs wrong. He probably was real happy to see his client is so competent."
>
> Dad with a stupid grin in his face, "Umut, if I know anything, I know people. He is threatened by my knowledge. Nobody wants a smart foreigner around them."
>
> I was angry with dad now, "dad, you are being paranoid."

> Dad with a stern look, "Umut, I am not being paranoid. To be honest with you, I think he is working with the I.N.S. to get us out of this country. If they can't get out us deported, I.N.S. realizes that a lot of people will loose their job over this."
>
> I was now angrier and it was directed to dad, "you are being paranoid. You think everything is a conspiracy? What is wrong with you? This is not Turkey. These things that you are talking about does not occur in this country. Quit being a stupid foreigner. This is America. This is the land of free."
>
> Dad smiled again, "sure it does."
>
> My anger grew and I said, "if you don't like the attorney just get a new one."
>
> Dad smiled and said, "you are twenty-four but naïve."

He did not have to say anything else, I knew what he meant. Changing attorneys in this short notice would cost us more money. Dad had already spent two thousand dollars on Mr. Jacobs on the second meeting. We were not rich. We were poor. We sure could not afford the luxuries of changing an attorney.

I could not sleep that night. I continually re-winded the conversation I had with dad in my mind over and over again. I could not believe the things he was saying. Surely he was being paranoid. Any men with that kind of stress would be paranoid. Then I thought to myself as I stared into darkness, "was he really being paranoid? Was he right?"

On December 8, 2002, everybody in the house got up real early. It was a Sunday. The whole family was heading to New Orleans that afternoon to stay the night there. Mom and Dad did not want to be late for the court proceedings following day. Everybody in the family was angry with somebody now. Mom was angry with dad. She continually blamed him for this.

> Mom screaming at dad, "if you would have paid the rent, this would have never happened."
>
> Dad, "maybe."
>
> Mom again screaming, "this is all you fault. Are you going to let them divide our family apart?"
>
> Dad just stared at her and said, "no!"

After screaming at Dad for a while, mom directed her anger at me.

Mom, "Umut, this whole situation is your fault."

I did not like her tone. I responded angrily, "how is it my fault?"

Mom, "it is your fault. You could have picked a better attorney."

I thought this was ludicrous, "you are a crazy lady."

Mom again, "it is all your fault. You wanted us to get deported from this country."

Another ludicrous comment, "you are crazy mom."

Mom would not stop yelling and screaming, "you wanted us to leave, so you could start your new life."

I could not think of anything to say to this. I was saddened by her comments. True at some point in my life that I wanted to live away from home. I wanted to get away from all the bullshit of being poor. I wanted to become a lawyer. However at no point I wanted my family to get deported. Nothing could be farther than the truth. I did not reply to her tongue-lashing. I knew she was mad. I could not do anything about it. No one could make her stop. All of the sudden the phone began to ring. I picked up the phone and said hello. It was the Brazil's in the other side of the receiver. Brazil's being the close friends of my family knew the whole story. Mrs. Brazil wanted to speak to Mom. They talked for several minutes and hung up.

Mom turned to all of us and said, "the Brazil's are going to New Orleans with us today."

This was extraordinary news. Mom had calmed down after the phone conversation with Mrs. Brazil. The news comforted mom. There would be people supporting us in the courtroom. Mom and Mrs. Brazil were good friends. The plan was that all of us would meet at the hotel by six that evening. My parents and my brothers loaded up in our little Mazda Protégé and took off for New Orleans. Brian Brazil would pick me up in an hour or so. I would be riding with Brian and his family. Our Protégé had five seats. Brazil's Buick was nice and comfortable. I would have rather rode with the Brazil's anyway. Let the foreigners ride with themselves. The ride to New Orleans would be peaceful. If I would have rode with my family, lord only knows how many fights would I have been part of.

The Brazil's and I left for New Orleans at five that evening. Mr. Creel, Brian's grandfather had broken his arm on his driveway around noon that afternoon. My parents had already left. I told the Brazil's, "if you don't go, my parents would understand." The Brazil's would not hear of it. Instead of leaving around noon, we left at five. Mrs. Brazil wanted to stop at Sam's in Slidell. By the time we left Slidell it was seven in the evening. The rest of the ride to New Orleans was real peaceful. Mr. and Mrs. Brazil were sitting in the front of the vehicle listening to music. Brian and I were in the back seat talking. We were oblivious to the things that were happening around us.

We stayed in Holiday Inn that night. While our parents slept, me, Brian, Kanat, Bulut toured Bourbon Street. We got back to our room at five that morning. We slept a couple of hours and got back up at seven. I was tired. Our parents were already awake. We had our breakfast at Macdonald's that morning. From their all nine of us walked to our court building. Mom and Dad were in their finest clothes. My brothers and I were wearing khakis. We got to the building at 8:30 a.m. our court proceeding would not start until nine. When we got to the lobby of the courtroom, the police officer asked my father, "are you an attorney?" My father replied, "no." My fathers suit had thrown the officer off. He assumed dad was an attorney. At 8:45 Mr. Jacobs showed up. He acknowledged our presence by nodding our way and walked through the metal detector.

    Mr. Jacobs, "hello Colonel Ozturk. How are you?"

    Dad replied, "I am doing well."

    Mr. Jacobs, "in the court room, you will be sitting next to me, while your family sits behind us."

    Dad, "okay."

    The police officer emerged from behind his desk, "all persons that has a hearing today please come in."

The lobby was full. Mexicans, Jamaicans, Americans (Brazil's) and off course Turks. Everybody got up one by one and started approaching the courtroom. As they enter the courtroom, police officer was marking their name on the master list.

    Police officer, "Kemal Ozturk, go in please. Fatma Ozturk, go in please. Kanat Ozturk, go in please. Bulut Ozturk, go in please."

The whole family went in. I looked around and I could not find Rain. Rain managed to sneak in with mother. The Brazil's had made their trip in to the courtroom also. Now it was my turn to go in.

> I approached the police officer, "can I go in?"
>
> Officer replied, "do you have any business in there?"
>
> I responded, "yes sir. My whole family is in there."
>
> Officer, "I can't let you in right now. The court room is too crowded."
>
> I tried not to lose my temper, "but, you let everyone else in. I am family member I should be let in."
>
> Officer, "listen to me, when somebody comes out, I will let you in."
>
> I was angry, "okay, thank you."

Ten minutes went by. I wanted to know what was going on inside. I continued on watching the courtroom door for someone to come out. Another five minutes went by. Still nobody came out. Another five minutes went by now. I could not wait any longer.

> I approached the police officer, "look buddy, I needed to be in there. If I am not in there, I am going to hear it from my mother. Do you have a mother?"
>
> Officer was confused, "yes."
>
> I reasoned with him, "if your family was getting deported, would she expect you to be in the court room or in the lobby?"
>
> Officer dumbly responded, "in the courtroom?"

He looked in the courtroom and found me spot. I walked in and sat down. The other people's cases were going on.

> Judge talking to an illegal alien, "do you wish to leave this country voluntarily?"
>
> Illegal alien, "yes sir."

All the illegal alien cases that occurred in the next thirty minutes were exactly alike. Do you wish to leave? Yes. Do you wish to leave? Yes. It seemed like an assembly line. The prosecutor would read the charges, the judge would listen then ask the illegal alien the same exact question over and over. I thought to myself I could be an immigration attorney, this is real easy.

It was our turn now. The charges were read by the judge, my family was asked how they were going to plead. Mom, Dad, Kanat and Bulut all stood up one by one, and pleaded not guilty. During the arraignment, Mr. and Mrs. Brazil had managed to sneak into the courtroom. After my family plead not guilty to all these charges. There was some mumbling in the back of the courtroom. It was Mr. Brazil. Mr. Brazil is a proud Irish-man with a quick wit and temper. Judge quickly became irritated by the noise in his courtroom and said, "what is going in the back?" This was Mr. Brazil's que, he stood up and defended my family with his entire Irish mite. Judge let this go on for several minutes and then stopped it. Our attorney was apparently embarrassed. That was it. All we had to say was not guilty.

Once the judge dismissed my family, our attorney and the Brazil's had an argument in the hallway. Mr. Jacobs told the Brazil's, "I don't want you coming back with the Ozturk's again." In response Mr. Brazil with a mocking tone said, "you couldn't drag us away from here." After the arraignment was over we went to eat at Landry's. We try to enjoy ourselves as much of possible but it did not work. We went back to the hotel gathered our belongings and headed back to Biloxi. Selfish bastard that I am, I did not ride back with my family again. I rode with the Brazil's. I was too embarrassed. I hated my father and mother. I did not want to be in the same car with bunch of freaking foreigners. Everything was their fault.

26

It had been two weeks since I.N.S. had paid a visit to us. They had showed up at our door to check up on us. The wanted to see if we escaped. Once I rationalized the whole I.N.S. episode I had forgotten about their last visit. I went on about my life as usual. I worked, played golf and slept. Nothing had changed. After I got off work on that Thursday night, sudden uneasiness came over me. The sky was clear with full of stars and the moon was full. Instead of being happy about life I was distraught. I could not rationalize why I was experiencing this mood swing. When I got home I took two Nyquil's and went to sleep.

Bang, bang, bang, bang, and bang…. I did not know what the hell was going on. I thought maybe the maintenance man was at the door, I went downstairs looked at the clock and it was seven in the morning.

>I opened our front door, "yes."

>It was the same two-asshole I.N.S. agents again, "where is your father?"

>I looked at them with total hatred; "he is in Minnesota!" This time I was sizing both of them up. I was real angry. I said to them, "don't you have anything better to do? Why don't you people go chase some real fucking illegal aliens?"

>I.N.S. barged in; "we are chasing the right people. Why don't you tell us, where your brothers are?"

>I responded with an attitude, "they are upstairs!"

>I.N.S. agents, "go wake them up!"

>The more I looked at these assholes angrier I was becoming, "why?"

>I.N.S., "none of your fucking business?"

I went upstairs woke Kanat and Bulut. By now mother was awake and coming downstairs too.

>Mother, "what is going on sir?"

>I.N.S., "we are arresting your two sons and taking them to Jail."

Mother visibly shaking now, "why?"

I.N.S., "because all of you people are getting send back to whatever hole you climbed out of."

Mother confused with her broken English was trying to reason with the I.N.S., "we are good people, my sons are good boys, we love this country very much."

I.N.S., "we don't care!" They turned to Kanat and Bulut, "put some clothes on."

Kanat and Bulut put their clothes on and came back downstairs. I.N.S. agents handcuffed both of them.

Mother in tears now with her broken English, "please don't take my boys away, they are good boys. They love this country very much."

I turned to these fucking Nazi's, "where are you taking them?"

I.N.S., "to New Orleans."

I realized the seriousness of the situation, and immediately changed my attitude towards these Nazis.

I said to them, "can we come?"

I.N.S. "you could do what ever the hell you want?"

With that they left our house. Mother was running around the house like a chicken with her head cut off. She was going nuts crying.

Mother shaking in trepidation, "why?"

I said, "I don't know!"

She called my father immediately. Crying over the phone, "they took our sons away, it is all your fault. You bastard it is your fault. I want a divorce."

Father, "go to New Orleans, call me from your cell phone."

Mother crying now, "it is all your fault. I want a divorce."

My mother had divorced my father over the phone. They had gotten off the phone now. It was my turn to make a phone call.

I called Mr. Brazil; "we need your help. Meet us at the shell station on Popps Ferry Road in fifteen minutes."

Mr. Brazil confused, "okay!"

Mother and I left the house immediately. We went straight to Biloxi Junior High School and checked Rain out from school.

Rain, "what is wrong?"

I said to her, "I.N.S. took Kanat and Bulut to New Orleans."

Rain was crying, "why?"

What was I supposed to say to a twelve-year old girl? How was I supposed to explain her that we were getting deported? For the second or third time in my life I was speechless. Once we got out of the school building, Rain saw mother sitting in the front seat. She started crying and running at the same time towards the car. At that precise second I knew I would never forget that moment. My heart was broken.

I got in the car turned to mother and Rain; "you must get a grip of yourselves. I can't handle both of you crying. Please shut up."

I know now looking back it sounds cruel, but what was I supposed to do. I was trying to be strong but I was torn inside. Twenty-five minutes later we made it to shell station. Brazil's were waiting for us. Mother crying got out of the car and ran towards Mrs. Brazil.

Mother, "Mrs. Nancy, they took my son's."

Brazil's immediately realized the severity of the situation. Mr. Brazil, "we are coming to New Orleans with you."

Mother was relieved that somebody was coming with us. Mrs. Brazil, mother and Rain rode with me. Mr. Brazil and Sean, his youngest boy was following us in their Buick.

During the ride mother would be quiet for a second then burst into tears frequently, "Mrs. Nancy, why my boys?"

Mrs. Nancy would respond the same way every time; "everything is going to be okay Gaye."

I listened to this redundant conversation the whole way to New Orleans. I was hurting inside. I was wondering now, what is going on? Is my brothers' okay? Why are they doing this to us? I decided to call father.

Father on the other line, "hello!"

My voice visibly cracking, "father, what is going on?"

Father calmly, "last month our appeal was denied. We lost."

I was shocked, "why didn't you tell us?"

Father, "I did not want to scare you and your brothers."

I was very quiet now, "so what is going to happen?"

Father, "I found us a very good attorney, we have ninety days to appeal the decision."

I was confused, "what is going on?"

Father was very calm, "here son, talk to our attorney."

I responded, "father it is almost seven-forty five. No attorney will be up this early."

Father responded, "I am at his office, here he is."

Another voice appeared on the receptor, "hello my name is Mr. Anthony, I am your attorney. Now listen to me carefully, I have filed all the required paper work in the past two weeks. You go to New Orleans and I will fax I.N.S. New Orleans office the necessary documents. Keep your cell phone on and I will keep in touch with you all day."

I responded, "thank you Mr. Anthony."

I was off the phone now. I was trying to picture what Mr. Anthony looked like in my head. He had a strong accent. I knew he was not from the south. I also knew he did not have a Yankee accent. I automatically pictured a foreign immigration attorney. It was nine o'clock now. We were in I.N.S.' New Orleans Office. I still had not explained anything to mother or Mrs. Brazil yet. I did not know what to say. I also did not want to get mother anymore angrier to my father.

27

At nine thirty, the six of us (mother, Rain, Mr. Brazil, Mrs. Nancy, Sean and me) were in front of a door on the eleventh floor of the immigration building. The sign on the door itself was scary, Office of Deportation and Detention. I was fully aware of the circumstances after reading this sign. The sign also stated the office hours and the bail hours. Bail hours were between seven in the morning, to one in the afternoon Monday through Fridays. I approached a little intercom system on the door and ringed the bell.

A woman inside answered, "hello, can I help you?"

I said, "yes, my name is Umut Ozturk and I am here to pick-up my brothers."

Woman inside replied, "someone will be with you soon sir."

I replied, "thank you."

All of us were waiting now. Mother was still crying and Rain was trying to console here. I was looking at Brazil's and realized how calm they were. I was mad at them. They did not know how lucky they were. They were American citizens; they would never go through things like this in their lifetime. I would have switched places with any American in a heartbeat. Needless to say, I was an unlucky fucking foreigner. No more denying it.

I turned to Mr. Brazil and Mrs. Nancy; "you have a pretty stupid family Mr. Brazil."

Brazil's were in total shock now, "what do you mean?"

I looked at him with a smile, "well if you would have picked your friends a little bit better, you would not be here right now with bunch of illegal aliens."

Mr. Brazil was a still a little shocked to my comment, "what!"

I turned to everybody and said, "you know that saying, show me your friends and I will show you what kind of person you are."

Mr. Brazil, "yeah."

I said to him, "out of everybody in Biloxi you picked bunch of foreigners to be friends with. You could have done better."

All of the sudden all of us were laughing in the lobby. The ice was broken. Even though everybody liked my joke, I was serious about my statement. I would have never made the same mistake as them. Fifteen minutes past by, I decided to ring the bell again.

Bell ringing, same woman answered, "hello."

I said to her, "miss we have been waiting to see my brothers for fifteen minutes now. Can you send someone that could help us."

Woman on the other side became a little aggravated, "sir, we will be with you when we are ready."

All of us just looked at each other. Deportation/Detention office door was locked. No one could have entered the room from the other side without a door swipe card. The lobby area of the eleventh floor had no chairs, just the six elevators three on each side going up and down. I was going crazy. Mother was worrying a little more now. It had been forty-five minutes since my last call. Overall we had been waiting in front of the elevators for an hour now. Finally Mr. Brazil got real angry.

Buzzer being rung by Mr. Brazil, same woman answered, "hello!"

Mr. Brazil with an attitude, "hello, my name is Marty Brazil I am here in the lobby to see Colonel Ozturk's boys."

The woman, "yes sir, someone will be right with you."

Another I.N.S. officer came out of the elevators. I had never seen him before. He turned to all of us and said hello. He seemed friendly. He opened the door of the deportation office and told us to have a seat in here and someone will be with you. To me this seemed like a giant step. We were inside now. After an hour, we were able to make it inside.

Mother crying still, "what are they doing to my boys? They are good boys. We love this country very much."

Mrs. Nancy, "everything is going to be alright Gaye."

Mother, "why my little boys?"

Mrs. Nancy, "don't worry Gaye everything is going to be alright Gaye. God will take care of everything."

Mother turned to me and said, "it is all your father's fault."

I looked at her and lied to her, "everything is going to be okay mom."

Mr. Brazil, "Gaye, I am going to make them pay for this."

Sean, "Ms. Gaye, everything is going to be okay. Don't worry."

Rain, "mom, everybody is going to be okay."

At that moment I was about to lose it all over again. Even though these people were family friends, who were they? How could they say everything is going to be okay? Off course they were going to say that. They were all Americans. Even Rain. None of them could really grasp the magnitude of what we were going through. Listening to their attempt to console mother made me sick to my stomach. I wanted to throw myself out of that eleventh floor window at the I.N.S. office. Purpose of my madness, maybe this way, I would make it to ten o'clock news and people will find out, how fucked up the whole immigration system is. No one cared! Only people that ever cared about us were Steve and the Brazil's. Nobody else gave a shit. However, I was not that brave to throw myself out of that window. I could have never killed myself. Even if I tried, with my twisted faith, I would survive the fall and be locked up in a mental institution.

Another hour had past. It was eleven thirty now. We were in this stupid building for two hours. We had accomplished nothing. There was total silence from the I.N.S. nobody came out to talk to us. Mr. Brazil got up angrily and started beating on one of the two doors in the detention lobby.

Big gentlemen with his badge around his neck answered sternly, "can I help you?"

Mr. Brazil angrily, "yes, we have been here for two hours now. I like to see Colonel Ozturk's son's."

Giant responded, "I don't know any Colonel Ozturk. I only know a Mr. Ozturk."

Mr. Brazil was a career military man; I could see his Irish blood flowing through his face, "that is Colonel Ozturk to you."

> Giant responded, "Mr. Ozturk is no longer in the military. So he is Mr. Ozturk to me."
>
> Mr. Brazil got meaner, "son I have been in the military for thirty-five years, once a person is commissioned, that person is an officer until the day that he dies."
>
> Giant responded angrier, "I am not your son. Mr. Ozturk is not an American officer."
>
> Mr. Brazil again, "son, officer getting commissioned is universal. Plus, Colonel Ozturk is a retired officer of a NATO nation, which is our allied."
>
> Apparently the giant was a last word freak; "we will get to Mr. Ozturk's kids when we feel like it."

I was thinking the whole time. Mr. Brazil is only making things worse. He came to help us and he is going to get himself locked up. I thought who gives a shit about their argument. I did not care if he called my father, "Mr. or Colonel." I just wanted to see my brothers and go home.

> Mr. Brazil changed the subject, "I know it is almost twelve now and on the door it says we have until one o'clock to bail these boys out. You guys wouldn't wait till one and then tell us, you can't bail the boys out, because it is too late."

Mr. Brazil had the last word. However, it did not help our cause. Another I.N.S. agent came into the room and everybody began shouting at Mr. Brazil. Mr. Brazil was shouting back as loud as possible. Sean and I were trying to hold him back. He had apparently touched a weak spot with these NAZIS.

> Giant was sweating like a pig, "old men, if you open your mouth one more time I will lock you up."

Nazis left the room. Mother was smiling for the second time today. She was happy her dear old American friends were fighting for her family. Another thirty minutes past by and the same Nazi agent that arrested my brothers showed up.

> Mother immediately saw him, "sir, can I see my sons?"
>
> Nazi, "no you may not."
>
> Mr. Brazil, "I like to bail them out."

Nazi, "you can not bail them out old men. They are not arrested. They are detainees."

Mother again, "I like to see my boys?"

Nazi, "lady, your boys are ours. We keep them here for ten days and then we will deport them back to Turkey?"

Mother hearing this immediately passed out. Mother started slipping out of her chair and the way she went. Mother was on the floor.

Rain was screaming now in fear, "mommy, mommy!"

Nazi turned to me and said, "you are next. Follow me."

I said, "okay."

As I started following him, my heart had made it to my throat. I wanted to cry. We started passing in front of the holding cells. Inmates were visible. Holding cells were made out of plastic glass. I was searching for a familiar face. I could not see my brothers. I was definitely scared shitless now. I had million different questions in my mind. What did they do to my brothers? Were they all right? Was mother okay? Was Rain okay? Was Mr. Brazil arrested?

28

BREAKING POINT (Friday 13th 2004)

I followed that Nazi in to a small room. The room was real messy. I thought maybe these people were living in this building, there was a small table in the middle of the room with a computer on it. There were bunch of folders on the table that were stacked up like the Sears Tower. There were also three visible old computers behind the table. Overall the room did not seem cozy at all.

Nazi, "close the door Ozturk."

I replied, "yes sir."

Nazi, "do you know why you are here?"

I replied, "no sir."

Nazi, "I am filling your brothers papers in order to get them sent back to Turkey."

I was more scared now, "why?"

Nazi with all the pleasure in the world, "because you guys are here illegally."

I said to him, "no sir, we are not."

Nazi, "we were going to let you and your brothers go back home until that old fool Mr. Brazil in the lobby made it worst for you."

I was definitely on the edge of my seat now, "how so?"

Nazi, "that guy Mr. Brazil and your father has pissed off a lot of people. He thinks he is helping you out but he is only getting us angrier."

I responded quickly, "sir, you can't hold me or my brothers accountable for someone else's words."

Nazi got on the edge of his seat and said, "hell I can't!"

I did not respond for a second and then I said to him, "when can we leave?"

Nazi, "oh no, you guys are not leaving today."

I said, "why?"

Nazi, "don't worry about it! Did you apply for your green card in Boston?"

I was totally baffled now where the hell did this question come from?, "no sir. I have never been to Boston."

Nazi pointed at a folder and said, "aren't you Umut Ozturk?"

I replied, "yes sir I am. But I have never applied for a green card in Boston."

Nazi started angrily moving his folders, "did you apply for a green card in Chicago?"

I replied again, "no sir, I did not. I have not been to Chicago in fifteen years. Sir with all the respect, don't you think there is more than one Umut Ozturk in United States?"

Nazi was totally outraged by this question, he started throwing his folders at me. I was about to piss in my pants. I got up out of my seat trying to dodge his best fast balls as good as I could. Nazi was screaming louder as he was tossing his papers, pencil and whatever else he could find at me, "you fucking foreigner, how dare you to mock me? Where is your fucking green card, you piece of shit? Who the fuck do you think you are? We are not in Biloxi anymore boy!"

At that second I realized, I should not say anything else. I put my head down as if I was a little kid that had just been punished by his parents. With all the commotion in the room a couple of more Nazi's walked in.

Nazi number two was a fat gentleman, "what the fuck is your problem Ozturk?"

I looked at him, did not reply and put my head back down again.

Nazi number three was another big jelly man, "Ozturk, you are just like your father. If your father would keep his mouth shut and played ball like he was supposed to, none of this would have happened."

This statement angered me, even though I was in total trepidation of these bastards. I found the courage to reply.

>I lifted my head up and said, "what do you mean?"

>Nazi number three, "you know what I mean, don't fucking play games with us."

>I did not know what he meant. With all the sincerity in the world, "what do you mean?"

>Nazi number three very angry now, "if your father would have shut his mouth from the beginning, none of this would have happened to your family. Instead he had to keep digging. Now his children will pay."

With that statement, I was in total disbelief. I thought if these guys wanted to keep us here forever, they would. I also thought to myself, "my father had done it again. This time he had pissed of all the wrong people. We had to pay."

>I looked at them and asked childishly, "are we going to be able to leave today?"

>My new friends were laughing as loud as they could in that room; they looked at me with happy faces and said, "no Ozturk, you pieces of shits are staying here today."

With that statement all three of them left the room to let me ponder in my thoughts. I was desperate now. The room was cold and I only had a tee shirt and my shorts on. I did not know what to do or say. Fifteen minutes went by and the angry Nazi came back.

>Nazi with a smile, "your mother passed out again."

>I said to him as calm as possible, "sir I am sorry if I mocked you earlier. But I was not trying to. Believe me I am not a condescending person."

>Nazi smiled again, "I know Ozturk!"

>I looked at him and said, "look, all we want to do today is to go home."

>Nazi smiled again, "Ozturk, you and your mother could go home but not your brothers."

>That statement felt like somebody had just cut my chest wide open, "why can I go?"

Nazi knew he was in control now, "you applied for your green card and they didn't. I also just denied your application for permanent residency. All I have to do now is to serve you with proper papers so you would appear in front of a judge in several months. Your brothers already appeared in front of a judge and they lost."

My wound on my chest was getting wider now, "why are you doing this to my family?"

Nazi with pleasure, "Ozturk, if your father only knew how to play the game, but he didn't."

I replied in a tired tone, "what game?"

Nazi smiled and said, "ask your father."

I was at his mercy now; "can I speak to my brothers?"

Nazi with a smile again, "no!"

My vision was beginning to get blurry; "I am not going home without them. Go talk to your supervisor and tell him, Ozturk wants to be locked up with his brothers. I am not going home, when my brothers are in jail."

Nazi was surprised now, "why Ozturk?"

I looked at him with teary eyes, "because if I go home with mother and she knows her sons are in jail, neither her nor I will make it through the night."

Nazi was getting pleasure out of torturing me, "what do you mean?"

I felt the tears rolling down my cheeks, "if I go home with mother, she will kill herself or her crying will kill me."

Another Nazi walked in again and said, "your mother passed out for the third time."

I looked at them both and said, "can I see her?"

Nazi with a wider smile now, "no!"

I was now furious, I stood up and said, "go tell your supervisor I want to stay in jail tonight and the next night and the night after that. I am not leaving without my brothers."

> Nazi started laughing, "Ozturk you are the first person that I ever met that wanted to stay in jail."

With that comment he got up and left the room laughing real loud. I was totally alone. I pulled my shirt over my head like a turtle would put his head in to his shell. I started crying as loud as I ever cried in my life. I knew they could see me crying through the glass window but I did not care. What else was I supposed to do? After five minutes of crying, I decided to pray. These were my exact words. Fucking assholes had broken me down. Gone was the sarcastic strong American male and replaced by a fucking sheep.

"Dear lord, I know I have asked you for a lot of stupid stuff in the past but this prayer is the one that I need an answer for. Lord, if I am your servant and you are my lord, get my family out of this building together and let us get back home. Thank you lord, I love you."

After the prayer, all of the sudden I had regained my composure. I did not know what happened but I was back. It was divine intervention. My mind had worked through the initial shock and was very similar to a car engine that had stalled and restarted. My mind was going five hundred miles an hour now. My only goal was to get out of this building as a family. I had to find a way. Five minutes later the Nazi entered in to the room.

> Nazi still smiling, "Ozturk, I talked to my supervisor about you staying in jail and he said no."

> I turned to the Nazi and said, "thank you for asking. But can you ask him another question for me?"

> Nazi, "it depends on the question."

> I looked at him and said, "what if you guys help us get our passports and we leave United States on our own?"

> Nazi with a sheepish grin was very interested now, "what do you mean?"

> Again, I looked at this bastard and said, "we leave on our own. You give us two months, help us with our passports and we leave this country on our own as a family."

> Nazi, "what if you run?"

> I looked at this mother-fucker that was trying to tear my family apart and said, "we won't run."

Nazi, "how can I be sure?"

I said to him, "you have my word."

Nazi was real happy about this sudden development, "if you run, we will find you."

I said to him again, "we won't run, you have my word."

Nazi was getting happier and calmer to the new news. How sad how transparent he was? Nazi, "does the rest of your family feel the same way as you?"

I said to him with a smile, "how should I know? I haven't been able to speak to them."

Nazi was so happy now, he did not mind my sarcasm, "you are right, I am going to go get them now."

With that one idea, he had gotten up and left the room to get my brothers and mother. I started kicking my own ass while he was gone, I thought why couldn't you think about this earlier you jack ass? I was real happy that I was going to see my brothers and mother again. Bulut and Kanat came in first.

I turned to them, "are you guys okay?"

Bulut's dark complexion was banana yellow now, "yeah!"

Kanat as pale as he can be now, "yeah!"

A minute later mother walked in to the room with Rain. Mother usually a very pretty young looking lady all of the sudden was looking like she was sixty. Seeing my family like this felt like someone was pouring salt on my open wound. I wanted to start crying again. However, I had to keep my composure.

Mother with her voice cracking, "is everybody okay."

Her question sounded as if a roll call, everybody nodded. However, she was not convinced.

Nazi, "Ozturk, do you have something to say?"

I asked, "can I explain myself in Turkish?"

Nazi nodded, "sure!"

I explained my brilliant idea to my family. I looked at Kanat and Bulut, "so what do you think?"

Kanat, "I don't want to stay in jail another minute."

Bulut agreeing, "me too."

Mother was the only one thinking differently, "what if we can't come-back to America? I love America."

Kanat angrily, "shut up mother, do you understand they won't let us out unless we do this?"

Bulut, "mom, shut up! I think you do want us to stay in jail."

Mother turned to the Nazi, "sir we love this country, why us?"

Nazi with pleasure evident on his face, "ask your husband?"

Bulut, "mom, if you don't shut up, I won't talk to you ever again."

Kanat, "shut up mother. We want to go home."

Nazi, "does everyone agree on leaving voluntarily."

Kanat, "yes sir."

Bulut, "yes sir, we don't want to stay in jail another second."

It was my turn, "yes sir, we are ready to leave this country voluntarily."

As I was saying those words I could see myself jumping out of the window. I was thinking the whole time why would I leave the only thing that I have ever loved? I was ashamed of myself for being so weak.

Nazi turned to mother, "what about you Mrs. Ozturk?"

Mother glared at all of her boys and said, "I will leave with my children."

With that comment, Nazi got up and went to check with his supervisor. His happiness was evident. Every since my idea, he had become much nicer. His attitude towards me had made a complete U-turn. As soon as he left the room there was a discussion in Turkish.

Mother, "I don't want to leave America."

Kanat, "neither do we."

Bulut, "you guys shut up. They are probably listening to our conversation. Argue when we get home."

Mother in tears now, "I won't leave, I will make sure my daughter grows up here."

Kanat, "mom, because of you, they are not going to let us go. Get a grip."

There was a silence in the room for next several minutes. I could not look at mother. I was too ashamed. Somehow, I felt like this was my own fault. If only I could have picked a better attorney. Nazi was back in the room with a smile.

Nazi, "my supervisor approved it. Ozturk, you have to be back Monday with these passport applications. It will take one month for you to get your Turkish passports from your embassy. After you receive them, we will give you another month to get your belongings together and leave on your own. Remember, if yourun we will find you."

We were freed to go. Just to make his point again, as we were following the Nazi out of the building he took us through the holding cell area. Once we reached the lobby Brazil's were waiting for us. No one said a word. I could tell everybody was waiting to get outside of the building before anything was said.

I did not say anything. I got into my car with my brothers. My mother and Rain were riding back with the Brazil's. In my own silent thoughts, I discovered how much that I loved my brothers and how I could never survive without them.

29

It was Saturday, August 20 2004. This was the first time in my life I was certain that I had to leave the great state of Mississippi. It was not that I wanted to leave but I was forced to leave. I had two options, first one off course was that I could stay and get forced out of America by being deported on November 18th. Second one was that my family and I would pack our house over night and leave for Minnesota. We had family there, uncles, grand mother, cousins, and nephews. Our attorney had instructed us to get out of Mississippi as soon as possible and off course my family and I had contemplated the idea since Friday 13th. On August 18th, we decided we would leave for Minnesota Friday August 20th. Besides our family only our close friends were aware of our trip. Steve was very upset. Brazil's stood by our side. We started sneaking our clothes into our cars that Wednesday evening. Whole house was agitated. But even worse the whole family was paranoid. Whole neighborhood had witnessed the arrest just a few days earlier. Every time we would go outside to put something else into our car we would see neighbors outside on their porch. My mom thought they would call I.N.S. on us. I could see her fear. I started looking around me every time I left the house. I had just watched <u>Enemy Of The State</u> with Will Smith and Gene Hackman. I became super paranoid. I continually wondered if someone was watching my every move. It drove me nuts. Next two days were the hardest in my life. Not because I was sad but I was paranoid. Whichever neighbor would look at me, I would wonder, "what if mother is right?"

Meanwhile, on Thursday mother had convinced Mrs. Brazil to ride with us to Minnesota. By Friday morning, my little brother had convinced my best friend Brian Brazil to join in on this once in a life time trip. Now we had three cars and seven people, my 1995 Explorer, Bulut's 1995 Sunfire, and Kanat's 2001 Protégé. Mother, Rain, Mrs. Brazil would ride in my explorer. Bulut and Brian would ride in Bulut's car and Kanat would drive by himself. We left Biloxi on August 20th at 1:30 p.m. I was the lead car and we would not stop for anything until we reached Tennessee. Each car had a cell phone. If something went wrong, the plan was that the other cars would continued the trip and meet at the first available rest area. If one of the cars did not make it the other would continue the journey to Minnesota. Our whole purpose on day one was to get out of Immigration Naturalization Services, Louisiana Jurisdiction. We drove straight up to northern Mississippi. We went through Tupelo and got to a Tennessee rest area at 10:30 p.m. We were out of the Louisiana Jurisdiction now. Nothing had gone wrong. However, mother wanted to keep driving all night and I didn't. I told her we would drive until Arkansas and find us a hotel room. Neither she liked my idea nor did my brothers. I did not want to argue with mother. I was very irritable. I said okay, we would continue on driving until I get tired. However around two thirty I decided to stop. Nobody argued. We stopped at Comfort Inn and stayed the night.

Next morning we loaded up and headed to our destination. We still had fourteen hours of driving to do. Morale in all of the cars were very high. We were no longer paranoid. Worst thing now that could possibly have happened to us was that we could get pulled over for a traffic violation. It did not happen. We went through Arkansas, Missouri, Illinois, Wisconsin and we were in Minnesota that night. If you never drove through this beautiful country of ours, I strongly urge you to do it at some point in your life. Everything was so amazing. Scenery was marvelous. America was beautiful.

30

We were in Minnesota on August 21st and on August 24th Kanat and I started working. My whole family and all the other Turkish people that lived in Minnesota worked for a gas station. It was owned by a couple of Lebanese guys. They were super rich. They owned twelve gas stations and they only hired foreigners. The reason they hired foreigners was because they did not have green cards or working social security cards. These foreigners would work hard and do anything for ten dollars an hour working sixty hours a week with no overtime benefits. They would never ask any questions. My uncle had gotten this job for us. Kanat and I were expected to work there. We had no choice. We needed to get two thousand dollars together to move out of our uncles house to our own. Meanwhile, Brian and Bulut were touring the city. Mrs. Brazil was calming my mother down constantly. Mother kept on itching. Doctor's had said her nerves were out of whack.

I started working at the gas station as soon as possible. I felt like a total loser. Over the years when my friends and roommates had made fun of those Arabs that had worked at 711's, I would just laugh with them. All those years I thought I was an American. Now life had played its biggest joke on me yet. It had thrown me a curve ball. I felt like mighty Casey at the bat striking out. Who knew? I was a foreigner after all. It took me exactly fourteen years of realizing that I was just another nameless foreigner. I hated who I was. I know self pity will get me nowhere in life. But this was the ultimate low. All those years I adjusted perfectly to this country and this culture. Why did I do this to myself? Why did I waste my time? I don't know.

I hated working at the gas station. I felt I was no longer in America. In the last fourteen years, I never worked with Turkish people; I did not know any. I did not work with any Lebanese or any Somalians either. Turkish people looked at me different. I could not communicate with my Turkish peers. They would get offended at everything I would say or do. Why? I don't know. None of my American friends were ever offended or ever as sensitive as these people. I was experiencing cultural shock. I was in America physically but I was in a foreign land mentally. I automatically shut down to everybody. I hated myself. I felt like Buckner going back into Shea Stadium. Even worse I felt like America did not want me here anymore. In my mind America did not love me anymore. I was jilted. I guess being jilted is what happens when you are in my family.

31

There are many nights I go to sleep thinking about Biloxi. I missed it. I missed Steve and the Brazil's. Granted I would talk to them on the phone several times a week. But it was not the same. I would have these crazy dreams that I would be driving down Pass Road and going in to the Keesler Air Force Base and being with my old childhood friends. During the dream my college roommates would show up. Then Steve and Brian would show up. Everybody would meet and we would be a one big happy family. In the dream we would laugh for no apparent reason for hours. I missed those days. I missed being happy.

32

01/04/05

A lot of things happened in the last several years. Let me recap, in the American League, Red Sox made a run in the playoffs with one of the greatest lines ever, "cowboy up!" Off course they lost and broke my heart. In the National League the curse of the Billy Goat continued its curse on the Cubs. Eventual champions Florida Marlins. In the NFL, Patriots won the super bowl after losing their first two games of the season. I was real happy. I am a big Patriots fan. You would think that I would like the Saints. No I can't stand the "Aints." In the NBA, Larry Brown of the Detroit Pistons finally won a title against the greatest sports franchise of all time Los Angeles Lakers. I guess I could say it was the year of the underdog. But the best news I could give you from the past two years is that my Boston Red Sox finally won the World Series.

During 2003, our deportation trial came and went. Our first attorney Mr. Jacobs did not say anything during the whole proceeding and it was the Black Sox scandal all over again. He was bought. The immigration court decided on my families' deportation. Off course we appealed it with a written brief. Then we lost the appeal without a lawyer. Finally we got a good attorney in 2004 and we are on our third appeal. The appeal process is still going on. It has been four years since I applied for my permanent residency and I still have not received my "green card".

33

America Hates Me, But I still love her!

I am twenty-seven years old. I have seen more discrimination by the United States government in the past three and half years that would last a life time for a lot of people. We will continue on fighting through this endeavor as a family. Am I disappointed? Off course! I sometimes wonder what ever happened to "give us your poor, your wretched, your huddle masses yearning to be free." I tell you what happened; now it reads NO VACANCY. "Have I lost faith in America?" No! I look at America as an ex-girlfriend that I am still in love with. She might not love me but she can't ever stop me from loving her.

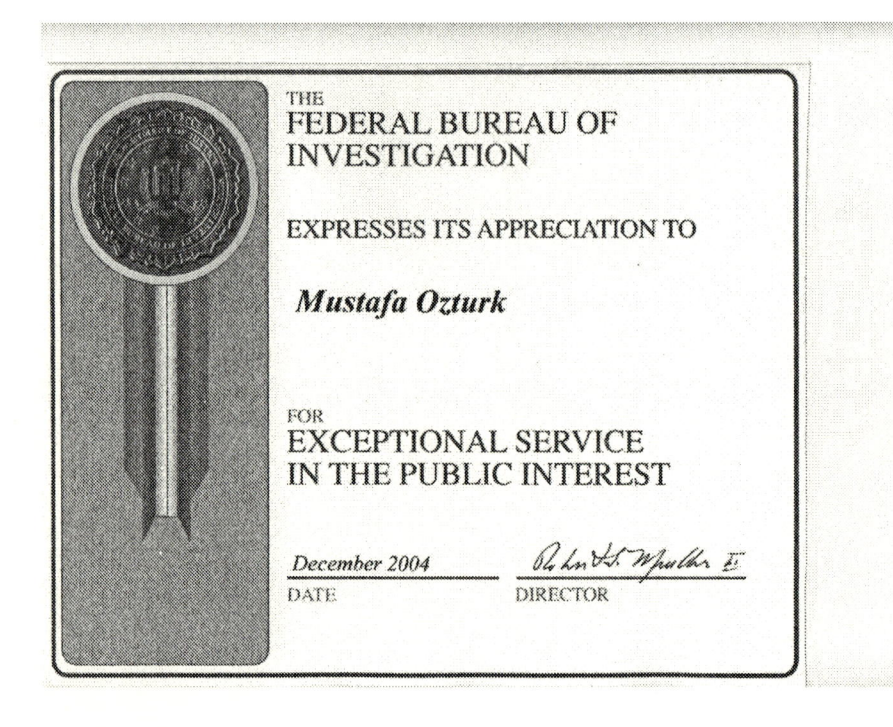

THE
FEDERAL BUREAU OF INVESTIGATION

EXPRESSES ITS APPRECIATION TO

Mustafa Ozturk

FOR
EXCEPTIONAL SERVICE IN THE PUBLIC INTEREST

December 2004
DATE   DIRECTOR

Printed in the United States
29687LVS00006B/40